"I'm Ha... Emery. ... Now."

Rob opened his arms wide, and Angelica slipped between them. His fingers twined together, low on her spine, and her hands circled his waist, completing a circle of love.

He kissed the top of her head. "You want commitment. I can't promise you forever."

"Promise me today and tonight." She lifted her chin until their eyes met. "We'll let the tomorrows take care of themselves."

He stared at her, wanting to believe his good fortune but deathly afraid he'd misunderstood her. "I have to go back to New York. My life's work is there."

"I know. And I also know that the old adage about absence making the heart grow fonder just isn't true."

His fingers brushed a windblown strand of hair back from her face. Glib reassurances withered on his tongue as he gazed into her eyes. "You aren't a woman a man could easily forget."

Dear Reader:

Spring is in the air! Birds are singing, flowers are blooming and thoughts are turning to love. Since springtime is such a romantic time, I'm happy to say that April's Silhouette Desires are the very essence of romance.

Now we didn't exactly plan it this way, but three of our books this month are connecting stories. *The Hidden Pearl* by Celeste Hamilton is part of **Aunt Eugenia's Treasures**. *Ladies' Man* by Raye Morgan ties into *Husband for Hire* (#434). And our *Man of the Month*, Garret Cagan in Ann Major's *Scandal's Child* ties into her successful **Children of Destiny** series.

I know many of you love connecting stories, but if you haven't read the "prequels" and spin-offs, please remember that each and every Silhouette Desire is a wonderful love story in its own right.

And don't miss our other April books: *King of the Mountain* by Joyce Thies, *Guilty Secrets* by Laura Leone and *Sunshine* by Jo Ann Algermissen!

Before I go, I have to say that I'd love to know what you think about our new covers. Please write in and let me know. I'm always curious about what the readers think—and I also believe that your thoughts are important.

Until next month,

Lucia Macro
Senior Editor

JO ANN ALGERMISSEN

SUNSHINE

SILHOUETTE *Desire*

Published by Silhouette Books New York

America's Publisher of Contemporary Romance

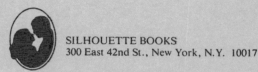

SILHOUETTE BOOKS
300 East 42nd St., New York, N.Y. 10017

ISBN: 0-373-05559-5

First Silhouette Books printing April 1990

Printed in the U.S.A.

JO ANN ALGERMISSEN

lives near the Atlantic Ocean, where she spends hours daydreaming to her heart's content. She remembers that as a youngster, she always had ''daydreams in class'' written on every report card. But she also follows the writer's creed: write what you know about. After twenty-five years of marriage, she has experienced love—how it is, how it can be and how it ought to be. Mrs. Algermissen has also written under a romanticized version of her maiden name, Anna Hudson.

One

So what do tame alligators eat?'' Rob Emery flicked the letter from his uncle's attorneys across his desk to his assistant. He kept the personal note his uncle had written tucked in the breast pocket of his pin-striped suit. "Cat food?"

Olivia skimmed the photocopy of his uncle's will, grinned and suggested, "Mike Lombardo?"

Six months ago, before he had landed the cat food commercial and had become the fastest rising star at Lockey, Stearnes and Cordell, Rob would have at least returned her smile. The mental picture of his rival for vice president of the ad agency caught in the toothy grin of a gator had the makings of being a drawing-board fantasy. But Rob hoped he didn't need to fantasize about Mike's demise. The partners would be announcing who they had chosen within the next twenty-four hours. Surely nothing would prevent Lockey, Stearnes and Cordell from making what he firmly believed to be the right choice—Rob Emery.

"Cats!" Rob snorted. "You aren't the only one who's having nightmares about them. I can still visualize the scene where the cat jumps off a ten-story building, legs stiffened straight out in all directions, lands unharmed on the sidewalk and struts to a bowl of cat food."

He'd pushed Olivia, the filming crew and himself to the edge of endurance to make damned certain the trick photography in the Jungle Cat Food commercial would make it a contender for the Clio Award. In an effort to top every urban cat lover's fantasy of owning miniature jaguars and lions, he'd demanded the animal trainers make the cats roam the paved streets of a New York City jungle in search of Jungle Cat Food. The series of sixty-second commercials rivaled the Indiana Jones movies for perilous stunts.

The less than cooperative cats and their trainers had been handsomely rewarded for their efforts, but Rob had felt as though he'd been dragged through a knothole backward.

"One series of cat food commercials and I'm ready to go on safari! I'm still picking cat fur off my clothing," Olivia said.

Rob grimaced. "How'd you like to have a farm that raises four-legged briefcases and purses dumped in your lap?"

"Thanks, but no thanks."

Rob barely heard Olivia's refusal; he was too busy thinking about Uncle Hogan. Why was this man, whom he'd not seen hide nor hair of in twenty years, suddenly disrupting his life? And why had Uncle Hogan decided to bequeath his house and farm in Florida to

Rob? Rob had been ten the last time his uncle mean-dered across the Emerys' paths.

Two decades separated Rob's mother, the baby of the family, from Hogan, the firstborn. Age and gender weren't their only differences. While Margaret had fit perfectly into the Mamie-Eisenhower-as-perfect-housewife mold of the fifties, Hogan was her antithe-sis, a flower child seeking world peace long before such a philosophy was popular. The moment Hogan "dropped in for a visit" with Rob and his parents, a visit that could last from two hours to six months, Rob could hear his mother grinding her teeth. Wisely, his father kept his opinion of Uncle Hogan to himself.

Rob had a sneaking suspicion his father had ad-mired Hogan Potter's footloose and fancy-free life-style. Rob could understand why his father, burdened with the responsibility for providing food, shelter and clothing for six kids, sometimes had a wistful expres-sion on his face when he looked at Hogan.

Wryly, Rob admitted to himself that as a kid he'd thought Uncle Hogan ranked right up there with time travel and a bag of nickels for the pinball machine. At thirty, he dealt with his misplaced admiration by firmly putting it in the pigeonhole where he'd tucked away his other childhood fantasies.

Much to Margaret's relief, Rob had outgrown be-lieving in Uncle Hogan's philosophy that the best things in life were free. The only thing free in today's world was poverty.

And yet, he mused, there was something about the contents of Hogan's letter that affected him like a ray of sunlight slicing through gray fog. Until he read the let-ter, he'd forgotten the day his uncle bought him an in-expensive box of watercolors, and the immense pleasure he'd felt when Hogan taught him how to use them. He'd forgotten how he'd felt warm all over when Hogan's antics had had him clutching his sides with laughter. And he'd forgotten how he'd glowed under Hogan's praise when he accomplished a feat by being the very best that he could be. Hogan's letter had brought those long-forgotten feelings out of the recesses of his memory.

Rob's brow furrowed as he recalled what had happened when Hogan departed and the paints were used up. When he asked his parents for another box of paints, they'd discouraged him from wasting his time doodling with colors. Gently, Margaret had told him how she wanted him to grow up to be like his father: responsible, hardworking, ambitious. She wanted a successful son, not a drifting tumbleweed like Uncle Hogan.

Olivia tapped her pencil on her pad, drawing Rob's attention back to the present. "The land might be worth something."

"Sure," Rob said randomly. Where had all those memories come from so suddenly? "Maybe I could put an ad in the real estate section of one of those holiday magazines you've hidden in your bottom desk drawer, for sale: alligator-infested swamp hole. Owner desperate to sell. No reasonable offer refused."

"You could give it away. Use it as a tax write-off." One glance at her boss's face told Olivia this suggestion wasn't going over well, either. "I guess there's only one thing left to do."

"What?"

"Go there and check it out. Who knows? It may be paradise lost."

"Or it could be Dante's *Inferno*, the fifth level," Rob muttered. *Paradiso*. "I'm up to my eyebrows making the right impression here, and Uncle Hogan's ghost comes chugging up in a motorboat!"

Olivia grinned and Rob's scowl darkened. She was supposed to be on his side. If he got a promotion and a pay hike, she would, too.

The intercom on his telephone chose that moment to buzz; Rob stabbed the button on the far right before the buzz ended.

"Emery," he growled succinctly. He seldom wasted time with a lengthier response.

"Come to my office. Pronto."

The line went dead.

"Great." Rob returned the phone to the cradle, pushed his chair back from the desk and jumped to his feet. "That was Earl Cordell. They must have made a decision."

"All right! Hong Kong here I come!"

Checking the Windsor knot of his tie to make certain it was squarely between the points of his white collar, then tugging at his shirt cuffs until they extended exactly one-quarter inch from the sleeves of his suit jacket, he strode briskly toward the door. "Don't book your reservations yet."

"You think Mike will get the promotion?" Olivia's disbelief raised the pitch of her voice higher than her arched eyebrow.

"They'll choose the man best suited for the job."

Olivia jumped to her feet to detain him. "You're it! Just remember to tell them I'd like a title, too. Executive assistant would do nicely."

Rob stepped from his office grinning at Olivia's audacity. Six years ago when she was assigned to him, inexperienced and lacking in self-confidence, she'd been simultaneously frightened and challenged by his reputation as an ambitious perfectionist. Time had erased her inexperience; success had elevated her self-esteem. His reputation hadn't changed one iota. As he weaved through the rows of desks toward Earl's outer office, the increased speed of the typists' fingers as they flew over the computer keys attested to that fact. If his heart hadn't been racing faster than a hundred words per minute, he'd have rewarded their increased productivity with a smile.

He wanted this promotion, badly. And he'd get it. Not Mike Lombardo, not Uncle Hogan, not a zillion "tame" alligators would stop him!

With that thought firmly in his mind, he took a deep breath to steady his nerves, then opened the door. Earl's secretary smiled, waving him on through to the inner office. Composing his facial expression into blandness, he knocked once, then entered.

Earl glanced up from his paperwork and motioned for his protégé to take a seat.

Bad sign, Rob thought, obeying the silent command. Earl was a great believer in the efficacy of physical contact: a firm handshake, a pat on the shoulder, a friendly hug. A businessman could set the tone of a meeting by doing any one of those three things.

"We're divided on who gets promoted," Earl announced without preliminaries. "Lockey abstained."

The muscles controlling Rob's lips tightened. As founder of the company, Lockey had the final say on most executive decisions. Rob forced his lips to move. "Why?"

"Mumbo jumbo," Earl snapped. "He knows you're the best qualified, the hardest worker, the most creative, but he says whoever gets the job will be under additional stress because of dealing with artistic temperaments and the media muckity-mucks.''

Rob's concern grew. Earl was obviously worried. Apparently the vote had resulted in a stalemate. Earl had backed Rob. Stearnes must have backed Lombardo.

"Frankly, I think the old man is going senile," Earl said. "That's the only logical explanation I can think of for his dingbat decision.''

"Which is?"

"He wants our top two account executives to take two weeks' vacation." The barrel of the pen he'd been holding snapped under the pressure of his fingers. "When you and Lombardo return, he's bringing in a psychiatrist to determine which one of you will—and I quote—'be able to tolerate the additional stress of the new position without suffering creative burnout.' To my way of thinking, we might as well send you to an astrologer or a witch doctor. It's all a bunch of hocus-pocus bull-roar!''

He shut up suddenly, apparently realizing what he'd said was nothing but nonsensical slang.

Rob mentally calculated the lost time Lockey's decree would impose on him. Two weeks. Fourteen days. Three hundred and thirty-six wasted hours. Just at the moment when he most needed to stay on top of things.

"Stearnes advised Lombardo to go to Hawaii. Sun, surf and sand. I hate to agree with *anything* Stearnes suggests, but a suntan wouldn't hurt your image, either.''

Conform, Rob silently ordered the perverse wild streak that threatened to explosively surface. Control yourself. Hold your temper, he silently coached.

His lips clamped shut, but his mind mutinied. They promised a decision by April 1! the rebel silently screamed. You meet *their* deadlines! Why can't they afford you the same courtesy!

He wondered what would happen if he showed Lockey, Stearnes and Cordell exactly what he thought of their indecisiveness by returning to his office and dictating a letter of resignation to Olivia!

Prudently, Rob squelched the urge. Two hundred thousand dollars a year was not the kind of money you played games with.

Earl had stood up and circled his desk. Now he clamped his hand on the younger man's shoulder. "I know you're disappointed. Hell, so am I. It's a shame Lockey is into this psychiatric tomfoolery, but I'm not worried."

He isn't worried; he's panicked, Rob conjectured. Earl's motive for choosing Rob wasn't entirely altruistic. The power plays between Earl and Stearnes were established fact. Each partner fancied himself as the ruling force when Lockey retired.

With a hearty slap on the back, Earl added, "You're the man for the job. Brilliant. Tough. Dedicated."

Rob looked up in time to see Earl glance at the mirror hanging on the wall over the credenza behind his desk. He's talking to himself and I'm considering throwing in the towel. Maybe Lockey wasn't the only one in the company going senile. At the moment, he wasn't too sure any of them had a monopoly on sanity.

Before he realized what he was saying, he blurted, "I'm going to Florida."

Earl beamed his approval.

Blinking, Rob tried to banish Uncle Hogan's ghostly image, which had superimposed itself on Earl's grinning face. He took the hand extended toward him as though it were a lifeline. It wasn't Earl's hand he felt; it was his uncle's, giving him the secret handshake they'd devised when Rob was a child.

Angelica Franklin stroked the silky fur of Figaro, the "attack" Siamese cat Hogan had given her, as she scrutinized the Langs' file. Pictures stapled to the corner vividly illustrated the differences between Tina Lang and her husband, Richard. Tina's snapshot had been taken at the beach; Richard's was a professional portrait taken by a well-known photographer.

Business uniform, she silently grumbled, noting everything in Richard's stiff pose from his impeccably tailored navy pin-striped suit to his wing-tipped shoes. Starched white shirt. Tie with teeny crests, twisted into a Windsor knot. Fingernails free of grit. Teeth perfectly bonded to create that all-American winning smile.

She shook her head, dropping the pictures on her desk. Her first inclination when she heard Richard complain about "mentally outgrowing his wife" had been to encourage him to slow down and catch up with Tina.

Paradoxical? Angelica mused. Not really. Richard had leapfrogged over his peers at work, but he'd become a social recluse. He'd physically aged. Worry lines marred his forehead; dark smudges under the eyes attested to his sleepless nights; pinched lips etched small lines around his mouth. Although Tina was tremendously concerned for her husband's mental and physical health, her sense of humor had prevailed when she told her husband that he gave the impression that his problem was severe constipation.

Grinning at Tina's irreverence, Angelica silently agreed with her earthy, but accurate, evaluation of her husband's appearance. Four years ago, Angelica's own countenance had elicited a similar diagnosis from Hogan.

"Hogan," she whispered, missing more than just his homespun wisdom. "God, I miss you, old friend."

At the mention of Hogan's name, Figaro lazily lifted her head and turned her gaze to the door. Uncurling her tail from around her body, she raised it straight up as she yawned and languorously stretched.

"No, Figaro. Lie still. He isn't coming back."

As though unable to accept Angelica's words, the cat narrowed her round blue eyes, and she clumsily leaped to the floor to see for herself. Hogan had always said he had chosen Figaro from a litter of six kittens because Figaro reminded him of himself: a critter who couldn't quite get it all together. A slow smile graced Angelica's lips when Figaro tilted her button nose upward as she sashayed toward the front windows.

In the past two years, since she quit practicing psychiatry at a private hospital in Orlando, Hogan had taught her how to laugh at her seemingly insurmountable problems. Laughter hadn't solved them, but it had put them in proper perspective. Hogan would have chided her unmercifully if he'd known how seldom she'd laughed since his death.

Automatically, she reached inside her center desk drawer for the cloth-bound book where she'd entered snippets of Hogan's homey philosophy. She traced the flowered pattern on the diary's cover as she recalled first meeting Hogan while she visited a patient in the geriatric wing of the hospital. She'd been worried then as to whether her article on mental hygiene would be published in a prestigious psychology journal. Although Hogan's unscientific, homespun theories would have appalled the journal's readers, they provided her with insights. Now she flipped through the pages until she found his exact words: "Laughter may or may not prevent ulcers, but it tastes sweeter and lasts longer than Tums."

Angelica's aqua-blue eyes misted as she closed the pages and held the book close to her heart. "Crazy old coot!"

His diagnosis, not hers. That was how he'd jokingly referred to himself, despite her efforts to convince him differently. In fact, the day she'd loaded him into her car and driven him home from the hospital, they'd heatedly argued the difference between being individualistic and being "crazy." Hogan might not have been a millionaire, but his alligator farm had provided money for the basics—food, shelter and clothing—and had left him the luxury of having the time to enjoy those basics with his friends. She'd returned to her apartment in Orlando wondering which one of them was "tetched in the head"!

She, too, had had the basics—frozen meals thawed and cooked in a microwave oven, a fancy apartment, a walk-in closet lined with drab business suits and snowy white laboratory coats. Any spare moments in her frantic schedule were spent contemplating her strategy to become the hospital's director of psychiatric services. She could count a multitude of professional acquaintances, but not one of them could she call a friend.

So who was abnormal? Which life-style was unnatural?

Those questions had prodded her into returning again and again to Hogan's home. Sometimes they just talked; more and more she came to help with the alligators. The bond of affection strengthened between her and Hogan. She had a friend, someone who cared about her well-being. After each visit, she returned to her apartment relaxed, but increasingly dissatisfied.

When Hogan volunteered to have a cabin constructed on his land for her to use as she pleased, she refused his generosity. She quickly discovered Hogan could be cantankerous when it suited him. He adamantly forbade her to deny him the fun of watching a new house "sprout" on his farm. She finally agreed and found her ambition to become director of psychiatric services seemed to dwindle in direct proportion to the increase of her interest in the new dwelling being erected a couple hundred yards from Hogan's home.

Once the house was completed, Hogan had planned an elaborate affair of making it a gift to her. To this day, she couldn't imagine where he'd bought a ribbon long enough to wrap around the entire house, or how he'd known she'd left work early to visit him unexpectedly—but he'd done both.

He had an uncanny sixth sense about those he loved. Instinctively, he seemed to know exactly when and exactly what his friends needed long before they thought of such needs.

Closing her eyes, Angelica recalled the Cheshire cat grin on Hogan's face when he cut the ribbon. He had clasped her hand to lead her into her new home, and at that precise moment she knew the answer to the question as to who was sane and who was caught up in a crazy life-style.

Within the month she'd resigned from the hospital and opened a private practice in Oviedo. Purposely, she restricted the number of patients she accepted, limiting her practice to families with teenagers in trouble and couples with marital problems, but they received thorough care, the best she could give them. Since prestige and material wealth were no longer her ultimate goals, she tailored her nominal fees to suit the income of her patients. Often, she worked for nothing other than the pleasure of being able to help another human being.

Hogan had gently nudged her toward self-fulfillment. Until his death, they'd been neighbors, friends and constant companions. It was no wonder there was a void in her life that Hogan had formerly filled.

"Gathering alligator eggs this year won't be the same without you, ol' buddy." As she placed the open diary on her desk, the pages turned to her last entry. "'Death's natural,'" she read, her voice thin and reedy, much like Hogan's voice when he'd spoken the words. His fingers had barely had the strength to squeeze hers when he'd added, " 'Don't cry. Celebrate. My next adventure will be grand...but I'll always be watching out for you.' "

Figaro weaved between her bare legs, purring at the sound of her voice, wanting to be held. Returning the diary to her middle drawer, Angelica bent and scooped Figaro into her arms, then crossed to the window opposite Hogan's home.

She should have been reviewing Shelley Cates's file, but thoughts of Hogan had distracted her. Tomorrow, she promised herself silently, she'd read through her Parent Effectiveness Training book for specific ideas to help Mr. and Mrs. Cates deal with their rebellious daughter.

As she stared out into the darkness, she saw eerie shafts of light flickering over Hogan's front porch.

"Some attack cat you are," she grumbled, holding Figaro closer to her chest. "I told you those beer cans I picked up meant uninvited guests were necking in our lane.... C'mon, cat, we're going to have to run those trespassers off Hogan's property."

Called to duty, Figaro squirmed from her arms and darted through her pet door before Angelica could decide exactly how she should go about getting rid of the trespassers. Calling the sheriff's department would be futile. By the time any officers arrived on the scene the mischief makers would have done their damage. She hated the idea of Hogan's empty house being vandalized. Of course, there was always the method Hogan had used a couple of times to frighten off rambunctious kids. Firecrackers! He'd armed her with a sack of firecrackers and a book of matches to use in just such an emergency.

"The idea," he'd said, grinning, "is to make the intruder think you're firin' a shotgun loaded with buckshot. Nobody, but nobody, especially a teenager, wants to be makin' explanations to their mama about what they were doin' while she's pickin' buckshot out of his backside."

For lack of a better idea, Angelica raced into the kitchen and swiftly located the sack Hogan had given her. Maybe, she thought, yelling at the intruder would be enough. She'd try that first; then, if worse came to worst, she'd resort to Hogan's tactics.

Careful to keep the screen door from slamming, she darted through the back door and circled the house until she was following the well-used path winding through the palmettos between the two houses.

The full moon broke from behind the clouds long enough to cast a monstrous-size shadow of the intruder on the front of Hogan's house. Her throat constricted in fright as she ducked behind a palmetto. If she could yell, which was probably physically impossible, this giant man wasn't going to be deterred. She sank her teeth in her bottom lip to halt its trembling.

He's no mischievous kid, she silently deduced, he's a full-grown man!

Gathering her courage, she pushed aside two fronds of the palmetto and peeked between them to see what the intruder was doing. The oak plank steps of the front porch groaned in protest as he took them one at a time. Her eyes widened as he focused his flashlight on the doorknob, rattled it, then muttered a mild expletive. She sank back on her haunches.

He didn't knock, so he had to know Hogan's house was deserted. The thought of a burglar ransacking Hogan's belongings sent a chill down her spine. She couldn't let that happen.

Dammit! Stop being a fraidycat and do something! she ordered herself. She opened the brown paper sack, reached inside and pulled out the book of matches and a string of firecrackers. Hogan! You'd better be up there watching out for me. This is your brainy idea!

Fingers trembling, Angelica separated one firecracker from the string, struck a match, lit the wick, then pitched it in the general direction of the porch. She'd barely plugged her ears with her fingers when she heard a muffled explosion.

Rob pivoted, pointing his flashlight's beam at his feet. A puff of smoke vanished into the sultry night air. "What the hell!"

"Warning shot, mister," Angelica called, dropping her voice an octave, praying the intruder would think she was a man. "Get out of here, fast, or I'll aim the next one higher."

Rob raised the beam of light toward the dense foliage, scanning it in a single sweep. When he realized the light made him a perfect target for the next shot, he clicked off his flashlight and hurdled the porch rail. Landing in a crouched position, he kept his head and shoulders lower than the fender of the Ford he'd rented while he planned his next move.

He wasn't about to drive back up that washboard lane and then search for a motel room. By damn, he'd planned on spending the night here, and that was precisely what he was going to do.

He'd survived the subways of New York City without being mugged or robbed, but his attempt to find rest and relaxation in the tranquil swamps of the St. Johns River seemed to have landed him in a shooting gallery. But he'd be damned if he was going to turn tail and leave. This was his land! Nobody was going to run him off it!

"Hogan, where are you when I need you?" Angelica mouthed. As though in answer, she heard a car door open and slam shut, then the engine starting. The firecracker had worked! Looking upward, she grinned and whispered, "I take back every argument I made about firecrackers, Hogan."

She waited several seconds, anxious to see the intruder backing up the lane. Why wasn't the car moving? She could have completely circled the house by now.

"You're wasting gas and polluting my air, fella," she shouted. "Go on! Git!"

The motor continued to run, but the car remained motionless.

She reached inside the brown sack and pulled out the entire string of firecrackers. If one little bang made the intruder get into his car, would a whole series of bangs motivate him to get the hell off Hogan's property?

Striking a match, she got up from her hunkered position to take aim.

The sight of a dark silhouette rising from the palmettos sent Rob catapulting toward his assailant. "Drop your goddamned gun!"

Angelica wheeled around. The match in her hand ignited a fuse just as arms of steel tackled her at the knees. The sound reasons she'd given Hogan for fireworks being banned in many states exploded in her mind as she pitched the lit firecrackers into the undergrowth while toppling to the ground from the force of her intruder's weight.

A long string of expletives coursed through Rob's mouth as the fireworks exploded. What kind of gun had fallen to the ground? An assault rifle? He'd watched enough *Miami Vice* programs to wonder if he'd stumbled into a smuggling operation. He rolled to the right, away from the spray of bullets, he hoped, taking his captive with him.

Sharp claws dug into his shoulders. A high-pitched shriek that sounded like a baby's was followed by the screams of a hysterical female, shouting, "Figaro." Their combined volume made the noise from the bullets faint in comparison.

Mad as hell, his ears ringing, Rob bounced to his feet and stared in complete shock at the woman curled into a ball with her fingers in her ears. Lord have mercy, he could have broken both her legs with his flying tackle.

Manhandling a woman, for *any* reason, was beyond the limits of his code of ethics.

He hunched down beside her and trailed his hands over her legs. A football player in his college days, he felt certain he could recognize a compound fracture if he felt one. While his hands thoroughly investigated the sleek calves of her legs and her slender thighs, his eyes warily searched the darkness for her partner.

"Stop it!" Angelica panted, ineffectually swatting at the hands sweeping up her bare thighs to the hem of her shorts. "The sheriff . . . will be here . . . any minute."

"Good!" Certain now he hadn't broken any of her bones, he rocked back on his heels. His eyes dared her to move one tiny muscle. "He can cart you and your partner in crime to the county jail!"

"Jail? Me? You're the one who's trespassing!"

"Keep your voice down." Thinking out loud, he added, "Her partner must still be around here somewhere."

"Partner?"

"Don't bother playing dumb," he whispered as he manacled one slender wrist with his hand and hauled his captive to her feet. "Come on out, Figaro! I've got your woman!"

From high overhead a puny "Meow," filtered through the leaves.

Angelica jerked her wrist downward where his finger and thumb met. "There's been a mistake."

"Yeah," Rob agreed, ignoring the cat's plaintive wail, "and you're the one who made it. Get your partner over here. Now!"

"Down here," she corrected and tilted her head backward to look in the branches of a century-old oak tree. "Here, Figaro. Come on, kitty, kitty, kitty."

Embarrassed for the second time within a matter of minutes, Rob took three steps backward and reassessed the situation. He'd tackled a woman, who did not after all have an assault rifle, and had mistaken her cat for her partner in a drug-running operation. But he couldn't have been mistaken about the gunshots or her warning. He'd heard them with his own ears—before he'd made a complete fool out of himself.

"Where'd you throw your gun?" he demanded in a valiant effort to save a piece of his male pride.

"Blown to smithereens."

"It self-destructed?" he asked skeptically.

Angelica's concern for Figaro's safety overrode her desire to make a lengthy explanation about firecrackers. "Could you give me a boost up to that first limb?"

"Why?"

"To get Figaro down," she replied succinctly.

"You're going to climb the tree to get the cat down?"

"She's afraid of heights because she's clumsy."

Rob raised his hands and took an additional two steps backward. "One of us has a definite problem. Up here," he added, touching his temple. "I'd blame it on jet lag, but I didn't cross any time zones getting here from New York."

Figaro began caterwauling in earnest.

"Look...Mr. Whoever-you-are, I told you I must have made a little mistake. I don't know why you were prowling around here in the middle of the night, but I've changed my mind about you being a burglar."

"Great. Just great!" Chunks of bark peppered his shoulders as Figaro attempted to move from her perch. He glanced upward. Cats weren't his favorite animals, but then, alligators weren't, either, and he'd flown a thousand miles to take care of them. Sincerely wishing he'd switched plane tickets with Mike, he muttered, "I'll get your damned cat down before it breaks its neck. You get the flashlight I dropped beside the car and shine it up there."

"Thanks. By the way, I'm Angelica Franklin." She'd have extended her hand toward him, but after he'd knocked her to the ground and thoroughly rolled around on top of her, she felt a handshake was a bit redundant. Instead, she flashed him a grin.

"Rob Emery."

"Your first name isn't job related, is it?" she teased, backing through the palmettos, turning when her backside bounced off his car, then circling around the front of it. Within seconds, she had located the flashlight.

"About as much as your name has anything to do with your being heaven-sent," he retorted.

Unoffended, Angelica focused the beam of light on the trunk of the tree; slowly she raised the tip of the flashlight until pink neon eyes lit the dark interior of the tree's branches. Perched on a bough, appearing totally unconcerned by her predicament, Figaro was daintily licking her front paws.

"Help's on the way, Figaro. Sit tight."

Rob mentally charted his course, then grabbed the lowest thick limb with his hands and pulled himself upward until he could wrap one leg over the branch. A sense of déjà vu gripped him. He'd done this before, only he hadn't been rescuing a cat then—his Uncle Hogan had been teaching him how to climb trees. Rob lifted his head, almost expecting to see Hogan, swinging his legs and grinning down at him, instructing him on where to find the next foothold.

Figaro stretched out on the limb toward him and meowed encouragement.

Angelica watched Rob balance his feet on the branch by bracing his back against the trunk of the tree. Carefully he rose upward. "What *are* you doing out here in the swamps during the middle of the night?"

Rob had been asking himself the same question when he heard the limb beneath his feet creak. His forced vacation was supposed to be giving him a breather from the stress he'd been under. If Earl could have crawled inside his head right then and read his thoughts, his boss would have switched his vote in Mike's favor. There was no way in the world Rob could have explained climbing a tree in the middle of the night to rescue some crazy cat! Never mind the part about the self-destructing attack rifle and the woman he'd thought was a dope runner. Earl wouldn't have listened to his lunatic ravings long enough even to hear about them.

"Did you hear me?" She turned the beam directly on him.

"Yeah, I heard you." He glanced down at her. The bright light momentarily blinded him, making him slightly dizzy. "Keep the light on the cat. I'm—"

Angelica swung the beam upward just in time to see Figaro lunge from the limb directly above Rob Emery's head.

"Figaro!" she gasped. "No!"

"Hogan's nephew," Rob finished, his head jerking upward as a flying mass of fur thudded against his chest. Reflexively, he caught Figaro and hugged her to his chest—exactly the way Hogan had caught and held him at the end of their tree-climbing adventure.

Two

You're Hogan's nephew?'' Angelica asked, her voice rising in disbelief. "You don't resemble Hogan. I don't suppose you have some sort of identification, do you?''

Rob scrambled down from the lowest limb none too gracefully, then held Figaro with one arm as he reached for the wallet in his back pocket with the other. "I can't believe I'm standing here in the middle of snake-infested bushes proving who I am,'' he muttered.

Automatically, she followed his movements with the flashlight, unconsciously noting his muscular arm, trim waist, narrow hips, but especially the pallor of his skin. Whatever exercise he did to keep in shape, he apparently did inside a building, she surmised.

"Oh, hell, my wallet is gone,'' Rob said, wondering what else could go wrong. "It must have fallen out of my back pocket while I was dodging your last volley of bullets.''

"Firecrackers," Angelica corrected as she swept the beam of light across the ground in search of his billfold. "And there aren't any snakes around here, either. The gators keep the smart snakes away—the dumb ones get eaten."

"That's a real comfort," he muttered, more concerned about slithering reptiles than his billfold or proving his identity. "While I'm writhing in pain from snakebite, I'll get great comfort from knowing the snake has a low IQ. Look, lady—"

"I am looking."

"Forget trying to find my wallet. It may be in the car. Trust me, I am Hogan's nephew—the heir to this godforsaken piece of land—and I'm also exhausted. It's after midnight. If alligators are like other animals, I'll be up at the crack of dawn feeding them. Do you think we could postpone this inquisition until tomorrow?"

His words and tone of voice told Angelica that he wasn't ecstatic about his inheritance. He also obviously didn't know the first thing about alligator farms. But what annoyed her most was his implied dismissal of Hogan.

"Come on, Figaro. It's Mr. Emery's bedtime," she snapped. Then she noticed the lines of fatigue etched around Rob's moss-green eyes. In a softer voice, she added, "I've kept the house clean, but the bed isn't made."

The cat, lightly kneading her claws in the mat of hair beneath her savior's shirt, wasn't the least bit interested in giving up her human scratching post. Rob plucked one front paw off his chest only to have it padding against the same spot while he pulled the other paw from his shirt. Figaro could be as cantankerous as Hogan when she set her mind to it.

Angelica moved closer to Rob. "Need some help?"

"I can manage alone," he answered, determined to extricate himself from Figaro's clutches without help. "Cat, you're an old reprobate just like Hogan."

Wide-eyed, Figaro relinquished her hold long enough to climb up Rob's front and lick her sandpaperish tongue along the line of his hard jaw. He grimaced, then straightened his arms with Figaro caught firmly between his hands.

From the way Rob held the cat at arm's length, Angelica gathered Hogan's nephew didn't share his uncle's love of Figaro or his property. She handed Rob the flashlight and wrapped her arm around the cat's middle.

"There's a key under the pot of impatiens on the front porch," she said, stroking Figaro's fur in atonement for Rob's disinterest. She thought about offering to let him use her spare bedroom, since she knew there weren't any sheets on Hogan's bed, but the scowl on his face made her decide a dignified retreat would be the wiser course. "I'm right next door if you need help with anything. I owe you one for retrieving Figaro. Thanks."

Rob's dark eyebrows drew together. "I was told I'd inherited Hogan's fifty-acre alligator farm. Do you own the adjoining property?"

"Nope." She ducked her head and rubbed her cheek against Figaro's neck. "Hogan owned the house I live in. I guess you own it now, huh?" She could feel her cheeks turn pink as the flashlight's beam trekked from her face to her toes and back up again. It didn't take a certified psychiatrist to read what was going on in his mind. Mortified, she added, "Hogan and I were friends. Good friends. I helped him with the gators and he helped me when I needed him."

Intrigued, Rob dipped the flashlight for a second look. She was mussed from being rolled on the ground, and a streak of sand clung tenaciously to her cheek, but it couldn't diminish the allure of the lush curve of her breasts or her long slender legs. Yeah, Rob decided, Hogan would have enjoyed having Angelica around, for whatever reason.

Rob had heard the emphasis she placed on the word *good*. He'd made enough mistakes for one night without increasing their number by jumping to another erroneous conclusion. Tomorrow, when he wasn't dead tired and covered with bits of oak bark, he'd sort out Angelica's relationship with Hogan. For the time being, all he wanted was a quick shower, a mattress and a pillow for his head.

Rubbing his jaw where Figaro had licked it, he gave a curt nod. "I'll walk you back to your place, then I'm going to hit the sack."

"Thanks, but I know the way in the dark." Let him add that to the other mistaken conclusions he's drawn, Angelica mused. Her mortification had quickly changed to self-righteous indignation. Evidently Hogan's live-and-let-live genes hadn't been passed on to his nephew.

She lifted her chin half an inch and swished aside the palmetto fronds between her and the narrow path leading to her house. Figaro climbed up on her shoulder and gave a sorrowful mew.

"Traitor. Can't you tell he isn't like Hogan?" she whispered against Figaro's ear. She lifted the cat off her shoulder and plopped her on the ground. "You can go back to him, but I don't think he wants you around here, either."

Figaro gazed into the darkness; she cocked her head to one side as she listened to the door shut at her previous home. Not one to be left outside at night, she turned and followed Angelica.

It somewhat soothed Angelica's ruffled spirits when Figaro fell into step behind her. "Smart cat," she muttered, wishing she could say the same for herself.

She should have realized that sooner or later someone would show up to claim Hogan's property. Since she hadn't been contacted by his attorneys, she'd incorrectly assumed Hogan had procrastinated about his will the same way he'd put off having a deed written for her house. Unfamiliar with legalities and grieving for the loss of her dearest friend, she hadn't thought about filing any sort of claim against Hogan's estate. Now, it would be difficult, if not impossible, to prove he'd ever given her the house.

There was little doubt in her mind Rob Emery could prove his identity, and his legal rights to her house.

"We might as well start packing," she grumbled, opening the screen door for Figaro. "Neither one of us made a great impression on Hogan's nephew."

Figaro gave Angelica a speak-for-yourself glance, then jumped onto the sofa and curled in to a contented ball.

"Maybe she's right," Angelica said with a small shrug. "If I'd scampered up the tree, he'd have left me there."

Too restless to consider going to bed, she crossed the living room into the kitchen. A cup of herbal tea would soothe her apprehensions.

Filling the teakettle, she set it on the stove and turned the burner on as she considered Rob Emery. Much as she would have liked to rattle through a list of abnormal psychological traits and have his actions prove him to be a perfect textbook case, she had to admit that for a man who claimed to be bone tired he'd behaved pretty normally.

He had thought he was being attacked. Apparently he'd believed she was there for some undisclosed sinister reason. From the twice-over he'd given her when she told him Hogan was just her good friend, he probably thought she was on his "godforsaken piece of land" setting up a house of ill-repute!

Angelica had to chuckle. Then she felt her cheeks flush as she remembered how he had looked at her. Not for permanent possession of Hogan's prize orchid specimens would she have admitted out loud to the peculiar sensations that had fluttered her heartbeat when his beam of light traveled over her as though she were a road map, pausing at each bump and curve.

"Rude so-and-so," she muttered as she removed a cup and saucer from the cupboard. That was the only flaw in his character she could barely justify. But on second thought, remembering how he'd volunteered to get Figaro and offered to walk her home, she couldn't support that defect, either.

The kettle began whistling as she pulled a tea ball from the drawer, measured in a tablespoon of home-blended herbal tea, dropped it in a cup and poured boiling water over it. Instantly the water turned a deep ruby red, the color of hibiscus flowers, while the aroma of orange peel, rose hips, lemon grass and peppermint filled the night's sultry air. When Hogan had shared his recipe, he'd said the fragrance alone made the effort it took to raise and gather the ingredients worthwhile. Angelica inhaled deeply in complete agreement.

Setting the kettle aside, she picked up the cup and saucer. She crossed to the old-fashioned oak pedestal table at the corner of the kitchen, where she seated herself. Elbows propped on the table, she sipped her tea, wondering if Rob had managed to find sheets and pillowcases or whether he'd collapsed across Hogan's feather bed without bothering with conventional refinements.

A pang of guilt sent a tremor through her fingers, almost causing her to spill her tea. She should have been more gracious. After all, he was Hogan's nephew, she silently reminded herself. He couldn't be all scowls and growls or Hogan wouldn't have made him his beneficiary.

Finishing the last swallow, she silently promised Hogan she'd be on her best behavior tomorrow. She'd explain who she was and what her relationship with Rob's uncle had been. And maybe, just maybe, she'd be able to coax a smile from Rob when he realized they'd both made mistakes tonight.

Maybe.

Rob's eyes sprang open as though they were venetian blinds being yanked upward. He flung back the sheet covering his naked body, grabbed the rumpled pair of slacks off the floor where he'd dropped them not five hours earlier and charged through the bedroom door. One leg in and one leg out of his britches, he hobbled across the living room swearing to wreak havoc on Angelica Franklin for daring to mow her lawn before the sun had risen to a respectable height. The roaring sounds that reverberated throughout the house were enough to wake the dead!

A zip and a snap later, he lunged off the porch, around his rented car and into the stretch of wilderness between the two houses. Muttering every curse word he could think of, he blamed Angelica for everything from the erotic dreams he'd endured throughout the night to Hogan's having bequeathed him this fifty-acre albatross that now hung around his neck.

Angry, unmindful of where he stepped or how tender his feet were, he located the path she'd taken last night and jogged toward her house. Once he located her it was going to give him great pleasure to wrap his hands around her slender neck and jerk her off the seat of her lawn mower. He'd never struck a woman, but he gave serious thought to bending her over his knee and pounding the living daylights out of her backside!

The path forked. He chose the most direct route. "Ow! What the hell!"

Through a red haze he glanced down at his foot. It felt as though one hundred tiny needles were lodged in his big toe. He propped his foot on the knee of his other leg and extracted a round, brownish-gray nubbin from the fleshy pad. Considering how angry he was, it surprised him that he'd noticed the pain. "Cockleburs!"

"Go back and take the other path," a call from behind Angelica's house directed him.

"She probably planted them last night to booby-trap me," he grumbled, glancing down at the creeping growth covering the path. After the explosive welcoming party that had greeted him he wouldn't put anything past her. Muttering to himself, he warily backtracked to the fork and proceeded down the less direct path to the right.

Outwardly, Angelica appeared to be calmly spritzing a bed of petunias and snapdragons with water, but appearances were deceiving. She'd risen before the crack of dawn in hopes of stopping Rob from venturing down to the alligator ponds alone. A mental picture of him throwing chicken feed and shouting, "Here gator, here gator," had awakened her with the first roar from down at the ponds.

She was also a bubbling caldron of questions. What did he plan to do with his inheritance? Would he move to Florida? If he planned on being an absentee land-lord, he had some definite problems, unless he'd made arrangements for someone to take over running the farm. When Hogan was alive, she'd helped him, and since his death she'd taken over for him, but her family practice wouldn't allow her to make alligator farming a profitable side income.

Having cleared the undergrowth, Rob picked up his speed. His head began to pound from the effects of a clenched jaw; his heart raced from exertion; the blood was roaring in his ears.

At thirty some-odd, despite his weight lifting, he was almost a physical wreck—and knew it.

He rounded the corner of the house bellowing, "Can't a guy get a decent night's sleep around here? Can't you mow your lawn ... later?"

He gulped; his Adam's apple bobbed. The sight of Angelica, dressed in short white shorts and a yellow-and-white-striped tank top, with a long expanse of shapely tanned legs and slender arms visible, had the same effect on him as a sharp jab in his solar plexus. It knocked the wind, and most definitely the anger, right out of him.

Angelica let go of the breath she'd been holding since Rob rounded the corner of the house. The sight of him had presented her with a major dilemma she hadn't faced since she was a teenager ogling the captain of the football team: should she keep her eyes on the dark mat of hair covering his masculine chest or watch the exotic green color of his eyes flare with interest as they swept over her?

A rush of hormones tingled her cheeks a rosy pink when she realized she'd given him as thorough an examination as he'd been giving her. Although Hogan had warned her never to tease a gator, her blue eyes sparkled with mischief as she said, "It's the mating season."

Stunned, Rob didn't connect the bellowing noises that had interrupted his sleep with her explanation. New York City women had a reputation for being bold and brash, but none of them had dared to baldly mention the fierce chemistry electrifying the air between them.

His head nodded, willing her to let her primitive nature run wild.

Angelica dropped the hose she'd been using and narrowed the gap between them. "I suppose you'd like to inspect what Hogan left you, hmm?"

Again his head bobbed. He sent a silent prayer of thanks upward to the heavens where Hogan had to have taken up permanent residency.

"Where would you like to start?" Completely unaware of the twists and turns of his wayward thoughts, she suggested, "The ponds?"

"The ponds," he affirmed, mentally replaying the fantasy every male has of a luscious woman enticing him into a Garden of Eden and making wild, abandoned love to him.

My God, he thought, this is too good to be true.

He blinked. He'd lived long enough to know that if something seemed too good to be true, it usually was.

He'd been in advertising too long to believe most of what his ears heard.

"Alligators don't have vocal cords," Angelica said to further explain the raucous noise coming from the direction in which they were headed. "But they announce their availability to female alligators by inhaling deeply and then, like a giant bellows, emitting a series of booming roars that can be heard for miles."

"It's the *alligators'* mating season," Rob stated, mentally kicking himself for letting his imagination run wild. "The roaring isn't lawn mowers."

Angelica chuckled. "They do sound like power mowers, now that you mention it. Actually, the bellowing serves a dual purpose. It attracts the females and warns other males to keep out of their territory." Side-stepping a small mound of grayish-colored sand, she cautioned, "Watch it."

He was. Following in her footsteps along the narrowing path, he scrutinized the provocative sway of her hips, the confident length of her stride that silently bespoke her knowledge of Hogan's land.

His land, he silently corrected, remembering once again that he was now the unwilling owner of an alligator farm. He didn't want it, he didn't need it, and the quicker he got rid of it the better off he'd be.

Hogan's generosity wasn't a blessing. It was a damned nuisance!

His hand grazed over his midsection to soothe what he called his permanent New-York-City-advertiser's-knot-in-the-stomach. He could feel beads of perspiration form on his upper lip. His breathing became rapid, shallow; his pulse raced.

He needed to be back in New York where he belonged.

Angelica glanced over her shoulder. The bright smile she'd intended to give him froze on her lips. As a psychiatrist, she was familiar with the symptoms of mental distress.

Slowing her pace, she asked, "Are you okay?"

"I'm fine." Her eyebrow lifting a fraction irritated him. "I'm a little out of shape, that's all. Let's just get on with the grand tour, okay? I don't have all day."

She saw him glance at his watch as he lengthened his stride to pass her. As he wore only his trousers and that wristwatch, she felt it was reasonable to assume Rob had awakened to the sounds of the bellowing alligators, pulled on his trousers and rushed over to her house. She felt it also safe to assume it hadn't been necessary for him to linger long enough to put on his watch.

"Type A," she mouthed, slowly shaking her head. Having been success oriented and competitive to the extreme when she first met Hogan, she recognized Rob's compelling drive to get ahead, to be a leader—even if being the leader meant going down an unfamiliar path to ponds filled with alligators!

She knew exactly what he needed to slow him down. Replace his negative worries with positive thoughts. With a light skipping step, she moved beside him. Giving him her brightest megawatt smile, she said, "I'm glad you're here, Rob. It's been lonely without Hogan."

Before he could respond, she wrapped her arms around his middle and gave him a giant-size bear hug. The touch of another human being is the most natural form of stress release, she told herself, giving him a second squeeze.

Three

His arms circled her shoulders reflexively. For him, to return her hug seemed as natural as for a man dying of thirst and sighting a bubbling pool of spring water to drink his fill. Whether he liked it or not, he realized Hogan's "good friend" felt wonderful in his arms.

"Friends?" Angelica asked, smiling up at him. "For Hogan's sake?"

Her smile warmed him inside, clear through to the bone marrow. He raised his hand to finger a tendril of blond silk the warm morning breeze had loosened from the barrette perched high on the crown of her head. Gently, he tucked the lock behind her ear. "Yeah. I'd like that."

Mesmerized by the tropical green eyes gazing down on her, Angelica felt a lump of emotion lodge in the back of her throat, as his hands framed her face. Without realizing what she was doing, she stood on tiptoe to move her face closer to his. Woman's intuition told her he wanted to kiss her. Later, she would analyze the compelling urge motivating her to be more than a passive participant.

A piercing bellow registered in Rob's mind as he began to lower his head. The mating season, he mused. Perhaps that explained his growing desire to sweep Angelica off her feet and carry her back to Hogan's cabin. Much as his traitorous body wanted to respond, he knew their fledgling friendship would wither if the fires of passion were stoked. Right now, he needed a friend a lot more than a lover, or so he told himself.

"The gators are calling," he whispered, his voice husky. Not willing to lose total physical contact with her, he trailed his fingers down her neck, shoulder, arm, until his hand held hers. "We'd better go."

Disappointment, sharper than a thousand alligators' teeth, caused her to gasp. Her id, the pleasure-seeking part of her mind, shrieked in rebellion, but her superego—the guardian that controls the id—sternly reminded her that Hogan's nephew needed her help, not a short-term emotional entanglement.

She forced her lips to smile in compliance. "That last bellow probably came from Arnold Schwarzenegger."

"You've named them?"

"Hogan did. He always had an irrepressible sense of humor." At the moment, explaining alligator behavior was decidedly preferable to dissecting the emotional upheaval of her response to Rob, so she continued hurriedly. "Gators do their fighting at mating season, so it's necessary to pen a couple of the bull gators to keep them from injuring other males. Schwarzenegger is twelve feet long and must weigh eight hundred pounds—a formidable opponent for amorous gators of lesser size.''

They passed through a gate of heavy chicken wire attached to wooden posts, then entered a stand of tall Australian pines set back from the spring-fed ponds. Here, in the dappled shade, a carpet of brown pine needles beneath his feet, Rob got his first glance at his legacy.

''See the mounds?'' Angelica asked, pointing at inconspicuous heaps of pine needles. ''They're gator nests.''

Eyes rounded in awe, Rob tried to count the mounds, each two feet high and five feet wide, and the alligators lying within fifteen feet of the nests. On the far side of the pond were separate pens for the rogue alligators. He estimated there had to be a hundred or more of the creatures!

''Under the pine needles is a moist compost of leaves and twigs that covers eggs a tad smaller than hens' eggs, but longer and usually rounded on each end. By fall, each nest will have about forty saurians in it—assuming they don't get eaten first by predators.''

''I can't imagine a living creature bold enough to take on a mama gator just to get scrambled eggs for breakfast.''

''Yeah, well...uh...'' Angelica stammered, searching for a polite means of clarifying exactly who the predators were.

''Yes?''

''Sometimes alligators are cannibalistic.'' Rushing on to keep him from dwelling on what most people considered to be a major flaw in the alligator life-style, she said, ''Hogan wasn't interested in raising the young. He collected the eggs and sold them to another farm in Silver Springs, where they hatched out. Selling the eggs isn't as profitable as selling the skins, but Hogan couldn't bring himself to slaughter his own.''

Listening intently to her melodic voice as she gave him a lecture in Alligator 101, Sexology and Survival, he stared at the reptiles basking lazily in the sun. Only a few of them sluggishly moved through the water. Their yellowish eyes and the swirling water behind them denoted their presence.

''Not exactly show-offs, are they?'' Rob said, not knowing what he'd expected, but certain from the movies he'd seen that the reptiles should be slithering into the water attacking some unsuspecting prey.

''Nope. They're fed regularly, which keeps them contented as milking cows.'' Angelica rolled her tongue in her cheek and impishly asked, ''Want me to run back to the cabin and get the camera?''

''What for?''

''Well, if you're looking for a little action, you could go over to Schwarzenegger's cage and pull his tail while I take a snap shot. Just think what your friends back home will think!''

''My bosses already suspect that I'm not playing with a full deck of cards. I don't need to prove it.'' A deep scowl furrowed his brow. ''When I get back to the Big Apple they're putting me through my paces with a shrink.''

''A psychiatrist,'' Angelica automatically corrected. The teasing lilt of her voice changed. ''Just what exactly do you do for a living?''

''Advertising. Lockey, Stearnes and Cordell. I'm up for promotion to vice president in charge of commercial filming... along with another guy who's been exiled to Hawaii on an imposed vacation.''

"Ahh," she responded as the missing pieces of Rob's psychological profile began to fall into place.

Now, she understood why he had arrived in the wee hours of the morning. He'd taken the red-eye flight out of New York City. She also had a grasp on why he wasn't thrilled about being his uncle's beneficiary. He was too ambitious, too anxiety ridden from grabbing for the next rung on the corporate ladder, to be concerned with what to do with a gator farm. Stress piled on more stress accounted for the fatigue lines, his jumpy behavior and his general crabbiness.

She opened her mouth to tell him that she was a doctor of psychiatric medicine, then quickly clamped it shut. She strongly suspected Rob Emery wouldn't take kindly to his new friend's being a "shrink."

She couldn't look at him for fear of revealing her secret as she asked, "So how long will you be here?"

"Two weeks." Rob scanned the fenced area beyond the pond. Used to summing up an adverse situation and making a quick decision, he asked, "What happens if I pull up the posts, roll up the wire and set them free?"

"Gators are territorial. Most of them would stay here and eventually die of starvation. Those that didn't stay would go searching for their next meal. Although they're naturally shy creatures, they'd become aggressive . . . a dangerous nuisance to your neighbors. Imagine being awakened by a choir of hungry gators in your backyard."

"Not a viable solution, huh?"

She shrugged. "As far as I know, nobody has ever stopped gator farming once they've started. You'd have to do some research on the subject. It's not something you can do on a whim."

"What amazes me is what makes someone start an alligator farm." His arm swung in a wide arc. "It isn't as though they're cuddly and cute, like puppies. And you can't stand on your front porch, like a wheat farmer, looking out over the land, admiring your handiwork." Truly baffled, he added, "I can't imagine how Hogan got involved with raising these big, ugly, cold-blooded, cannibalistic beasts."

"Hogan didn't see them in that light. Nor do I," she said, to set the record straight. She seldom climbed up on a soapbox for another man's cause, but Hogan wasn't here to speak for himself. She'd have to do it for him. "Thirty years ago alligators were on the endangered species list. It's because of people like Hogan, people who cared about the world where they lived, that they didn't meet the same fate as the passenger pigeons."

"That was thirty years ago. The pendulum has swung in the other direction, hasn't it? Isn't there an alligator season in Florida?"

She nodded. "But that doesn't mean gators are no longer valuable."

On the receiving end of Rob's skeptical glance, she knew she hadn't convinced him of the alligator's worth. A New York advertising executive wasn't swayed by emotional arguments. The disdain clearly visible on Rob's face told her she had to try another tactic.

"Commercially, their hides are *extremely* valuable. Think about how much you city folks pay for a billfold or a briefcase that's made of alligator skin."

"I could sell them, couldn't I?" Rob inquired, finding a simple solution to his problem. No alligators. No responsibility down here, he silently mused. Sell the alligators. Sell the land. Poof! I'm back in New York where I belong.

Angelica looked him square in the eye. "Slaughter them? You'd do that?"

"Not me specifically. I'd hire someone to do it."

"Oh, that makes it better," she replied sarcastically, totally forgetting about their friendship or his stressed-out psyche. "You wouldn't want the *cold* blood of Hogan's *beasts* to dirty those lily-white hands of yours, would you?"

She turned on her heel and marched back toward the gate.

"Wait a minute, Angelica," he called. "It was only an idea."

"A lousy idea. Hogan is probably spinning in his grave right now. That idea probably doesn't bother you, either!"

"Where are you going in such an all-fired hurry?"

"Home. I'm going to find Figaro before you start getting ideas about her!"

"Dammit! You're being unreasonable! If I can't set them free and I can't slaughter them, what the hell do you think I should do with them!" When he saw her pick up her pace to a steady jog, he shouted, "The least you could do is show me how to feed them."

Angelica whirled around. "Go jump in the lake, buster! That'll take care of your problems and theirs!"

Not about either to take her advice or to be left standing alone on the banks of an alligator pond, Rob sprinted after her. "What's Hogan going to think if you don't help me feed them?"

"He's going to think it's one of the days they aren't supposed to be fed."

"Oh." How the hell was he supposed to know they weren't fed every day? He'd heard tales of alligators living in the sewers in New York City, but he wasn't their keeper! "You could have told me that earlier."

"When? When you knocked me down and shoved my face in the sand? When you came roaring over this morning screaming about lawn mowers? From now on, *friend*, you wanna know something, you ask—politely."

To pacify her, he inquired, "Do you happen to have any books about alligator farming you'd be willing to lend me?" The long curls clustered at the back of her head bounced up and down on her nape as she nodded, but Rob would have wagered his end-of-the-year bonus that those kissable lips of hers remained in a stubborn straight line. A cold spot deep inside of him needed the warmth of her smile. To earn it, he said, "If I'm going to wrestle gators, I'd better learn how to keep them fit for battle."

An image of him rolling around with Schwarzenegger tweaked her sense of humor. Rob needed to learn how to keep himself fit!

Through a web of long dark eyelashes, she furtively glanced over her shoulder at Rob. He'd teased her, but he wasn't smiling. Come to think of it, she'd yet to see him smile or chuckle or laugh.

Angelica paused at the gate, waiting for him to catch up with her. She wondered if sometime during his corporate career he'd purposely had his sense of humor removed—thinking that like an appendix, it wasn't needed so why have it? No wonder he was so jumpy.

His decision to dump Hogan's property posthaste and depart was all wrong. What he really needed to do was follow the advice Hogan had given her: stop and smell the sunshine.

She reached up and unlooped the wire holding the posts together. Hogan had also said something about men who made hard and fast decisions. What was it? Her smile broadened as she recalled his exact words: Every little girl should learn that a man who's worth his salt makes a decision and sticks by it—until a woman shows him pleasant alternatives.

Rob had made up his mind to dump Hogan's property; it was up to her to make him see other options.

She pushed against the gate, preceded him through the opening, then turned to refasten the wire. Rob had taken care of securing it.

"Could I interest you in a pot of freshly brewed coffee to go along with the books you want to borrow?" she offered.

"How about my fixing you a cup of coffee?" He didn't know diddly-squat about alligators, but he could brew a wicked cup of coffee.

Angelica wasn't a woman who held a grudge for more than ten minutes. Immensely pleased by his invitation, she accepted by offering him her hand. Rob gladly took it.

"Ready to answer the burning question that's been bothering me since I was notified of my legacy?"

His thumb was absentmindedly brushing across her knuckles, sending tiny sparks of energy up her arm. Angelica's voice was husky as she replied, "Sure."

"What do *tame* alligators eat? And how much?"

"That varies according to the temperature." Her temperature was rising faster than the sun overhead. To still her response to his slightest touch, she answered, "During the cold months, when their heartbeat can be as slow as one beat per minute, they only eat once a week, or less, depending on the severity of the cold snap. When the weather warms up, they're fed once a day to curb their...undesirable nature. In captivity their diet consists of raw meat—such as fish or chicken heads—which are fortified with vitamins.''

"Gross."

"Cheap and nutritious."

"What do they *like* to eat—other than snakes?"

"Fish. Unwary birds. Small animals." She could tell he wasn't delighted with that response, either. "What'd you expect to feed them? T-bone steaks and chateau-briand?''

"I was hoping we could teach them to eat cat food."

"Why cat food?"

"Because one of my clients manufactures cat food. Imagine how the reports would read if sales in Florida zoomed sky-high after the commercial we just finished hits prime time on the television screen." His lips tilted at the corners in a grimace of a smile. "I'd be a shoo-in for vice president, regardless of what the shrink has to say."

Once again Angelica felt compelled to tell him what she did for a living, but a mound of ants prevented it. "Watch where you...step!" His bare foot had landed smack-dab in the mound before she could push him aside.

"Ants. No big deal. We have them back in New York, too."

He'd stepped on the edge of the mound and taken several more steps before the little devils silently communicated to one another, "Sic him!"

Angelica shook her hand loose from his and dropped to one knee, brushing her hand across his toes. "Fire ants."

Jerking up his pant leg, Rob began furiously swatting at them. "Those little demons pack a mean sting! Gotcha!"

For every "gotcha" Angelica heard, she knew the ones he hadn't gotten were seeking revenge.

"They're climbing up my pant legs." His jaw hardened; his green eyes widened. He slapped at his upper thigh. "Ouch! Damn!"

From the expression on his face, she knew he wanted to shuck his britches, but her presence prevented such a course of action.

"I'll meet you at Hogan's cabin!"

She shouldn't have chuckled, but his stricken expression and his comical flight down the path reminded her of a kid slapping his haunches while he pretended to be riding a horse lickety-split. Those mite-size critters had taken the swagger right out of his walk.

"Just ants," she repeated, mimicking the arrogant tone of his voice. "The next time he's outside I'll have to put a board down his back to keep his eyes off the ground!"

Rising to her feet, she lifted her face to the sun, swung her arms wide, then hugged herself. With a gleeful hop, skip and jump, she started toward Rob's house. She felt gloriously alive. Melancholy and loneliness had vanished with Rob's arrival.

He wasn't Hogan—no one could ever replace him— but deep inside she knew Rob was special.

"Just ants," Rob muttered, stepping from the shower stall, grabbing a towel from the linen closet and efficiently wiping up the rivulets of water dripping from his wet hair. He checked to make certain he'd gotten rid of all of them. "Miniature hornets!"

He wrapped the towel around his waist and crossed to the medicine cabinet behind the mirror. Automatically, his fingers raked over his unshaved jaw before he opened the cabinet. He needed a shave, but he needed to put some ointment on his injuries. He didn't know if he'd been bitten or stung; from the red marks peppering his legs and feet, he suspected both had occurred.

Judging from the shortage of medication in Hogan's cabinet he deduced that his uncle had been seldom ill and had stayed away from fire ants. He reached for the unopened bottle of calamine lotion, wishing for something stronger. His own medicine cabinet resembled a well-stocked drugstore. There had been days when modern medicine was the only thing between his staying in bed sick and missing a day of work and dragging himself to the office.

He lowered the lid on the toilet seat, sat down and diligently began coating each red mark with dots of pink lotion. His big toe looked like pink polka-dotted ribbon within seconds. Impatient with the tedious chore, he trickled the medicine directly on his shin and rubbed downward.

There was a rap on the screen door that led in from the front porch. "Rob?"

"Yeah. Come on in and make yourself at home." Standing, he eyed his crumpled slacks. He hitched the towel snugly around his waist. He wasn't about to risk wearing the same slacks. In fact, he wanted them fumigated before he'd consider wearing them. That left him with a problem—his clothes were still in his suitcase, down the hallway in the bedroom, in full view of anyone standing in the kitchen. "I'll be out in a minute."

"I'll start the coffee."

An *un*liberated woman? Rob mused, almost grinning. "Help yourself. Mind if I take time to shave?"

Mind if I come and watch? Angelica wanted to ask. The masculine ritual of shaving had always fascinated her. An image of thick soapy lather beneath bright eyes the color of rain-doused gardenia leaves had her dragging her hands down the side seams of her shorts. Propriety made her call, "No. Go ahead."

Rob opened the cabinet under the sink to look for Hogan's shaving gear. Uh-uh, he thought, glancing at a straight razor and shaving mug. He'd pluck his whiskers one by one before he took a chance on slitting his throat. Mike Lombardo wasn't going to get the vice presidency by default.

"Angelica, would you bring me my shaving kit and a pair of shorts? They're in the suitcase in the bedroom."

The heaping spoonful of ground coffee spilled into the paper filter. Primitive vibrations had not caused her hand to shake, she staunchly denied. The thought of going through his suitcase and picking out the clothing he'd be wearing didn't affect her one way or another. Or so she told herself as she blithely answered, "Sure thing."

She set the measuring spoon in the sink, then strode from the kitchen to the bedroom. She refused to notice that he had not taken time to make the bed last night or that the imprint of his body had left a curved hollow in the middle of the feather mattress. Nor did she notice how tossed and rumpled the bedclothes were. Of course she didn't. She wasn't interested in which side of the bed he'd slept on or whether he'd had a restful night's sleep.

One hard yank and she had Rob's suitcase in the middle of Hogan's big brass bed. She flicked the latches, feeling as though she were opening Pandora's box. She did notice how neatly he'd folded and packed his clothing: shirts and tennis shorts alternating on top to the right, trousers on the bottom, and, nestled around his shaving kit, delightfully scandalous-sized underwear to the left.

A smile quirked her lips as she picked up a pair of navy-blue briefs between her thumbs and forefingers. "My, my, my," she murmured, stretching the waistband, then softly whistling between her teeth. "There must be something Freudian about these!"

"Angelica! The water's boiling. The kettle's whistling."

"Coming!"

Holding on to his underwear with one hand, she snatched the shaving kit and the top two articles of clothing with the other. The shorts could have been plaid and the shirt striped; she wouldn't have noticed. Fortunately for her, Rob had stacked coordinating outfits in order when he packed.

She hurried through the door toward the bathroom. The piercing whistle coming from the kitchen reassured her that he hadn't overheard her appreciative whistle. She shoved his clothes into the hand dangling outside the bathroom door and beat a hasty retreat into the kitchen.

She needed a strong cup of coffee, badly. The first thing she planned on doing when she returned to her house was to gather up her reading materials on repression, denial and rampant female hormones. Psychologically, there had to be some factor motivating her keen interest in every intimate detail of Rob Emery's wardrobe.

Minutes later, she sat drinking coffee in a nonchalant pose—elbows propped on the dinette table, one foot curled under her and one swinging free—as Rob sauntered into the room. She wasn't going to let him know he had an unholy effect on her nervous system until she figured out precisely what caused it.

"Smells terrific," he commented, before taking a sip. "Ahh, yes. You brew a fine cup of coffee, Ms. Fairbanks."

Although her coffee cup remained directly beneath her nose, all Angelica smelled was Old Spice aftershave. Her toes curled—something that hadn't happened when Hogan had worn the same fragrance.

Through lowered lashes she slowly surveyed him while he settled into the chair across from her. Cleanshaven, hair slicked back in place and without his perpetual scowl, he could have qualified as a model for the advertising agency where he worked.

"I guess you've been wondering why Hogan chose me as his beneficiary?"

"The question did cross my mind," she replied honestly. Her eyes dropped to a broad red stripe on his chest where a navy-blue polo player sat astride a galloping horse. "Hogan rarely spoke of his relatives."

"What you mean is he didn't have anything nice to say, so he kept his mouth shut?"

Angelica's unpremeditated grin made denying his statement pointless. "He did mention his sister. Once."

"My mother. Twenty-one years' difference in age probably accounted for neither one of them understanding the other. I suppose Hogan, being the older, tried to breach the generation gap. Pardon my speaking bluntly, but my mother had strong reservations against taking advice from an aging ne'er-do-well.''

"How did you feel about him?"

Rob paused, drinking his coffee, analyzing exactly how he did feel about his uncle. "As a child...enthralled. He could take a matchstick, a button, a rubber band and an empty spool of thread and make self-propelling cars. He could puff up his cheek and hold his breath until... well, it seemed like forever back then. And he could paint fantasy pictures of mythical dragons and knights on chargers while he told adventure stories.''

"I've seen some of his watercolors. He was very talented.''

"Mother said he could have been an illustrator for children's books, held down a respectable job and earned a decent living.''

Angelica grinned. She knew exactly what Hogan had done with his paintings. "He gave them away to your neighborhood playmates.''

"How did you know?"

"Hogan wasn't interested in earning money for doing something that gave him joy.''

He'd given her a painting of a young woman, with her waist-long hair hanging loose, dressed in a diaphanous gown that swirled around her as she twirled beneath gossamer moonbeams in a thicket of tropical splendor. That was how he'd pictured she would be, once she found true happiness. He'd hung it in her bedroom and guaranteed sweet dreams if she looked at it each night before she went to sleep.

"Which gives credence to Mother's opinion that he was shiftless, lazy and just a touch crazy. Needless to say, she didn't like my idolizing him."

Tongue-in-cheek, she asked, "Your mother didn't want a son who worked only when he needed money for necessities?"

Rob shook his head. "No more than she liked Hogan wandering in and out of our lives like a sleepwalker. No one knew when he'd arrive and no one knew when he'd depart. The last time I saw him I was twelve. He bought me a set of watercolors, taught me the rudiments, then told me he was about to embark on a grand adventure. He was going to paradise—Florida—to search for the fountain of youth."

For a fraction of a second, she thought Rob smiled, then decided she must have been wrong. In the blink of an eye, his stern mask was back in place.

"Hero or bum?" he murmured, not able to answer his own question. "Mythical or mortal?"

"In my book, he was a hero. Perhaps he's immortal, too. Hogan believed a man attained immortality by being alive in the hearts and souls of his friends."

Rob shot her a peculiar look. "Next you'll be telling me he really did have a sixth sense about what took place in other people's lives."

"He did have an uncanny sense of knowing when someone needed something, before the person involved knew it."

Instantly, Angelica had an insight into why Hogan's having left Rob the gator farm bothered him. Rob considered himself within grasping distance of success. If Hogan's sixth sense had led him to leave Rob a piece of property in Florida, that meant Rob was vulnerable. He could fail to get the vice presidency he so avidly sought.

The merest possibility of failure scared the hell out of Rob.

Rob had to get rid of the farm and return to New York to prove to himself that Hogan's sixth sense was wrong, that he wouldn't fail.

Their eyes met at the roadblock of their mutual thoughts. There was a moment's more silence before Rob spoke.

"The letter Hogan sent me was..." His voice trailed into nothingness as he searched for the right phrase to express how the letter had made him feel, apart from the fact that it came from a man who'd been dead for weeks. Unable to find a more appropriate word, he said, "Spooky."

"Spooky?"

"Yeah. I felt like Charles Dickens's Scrooge being visited by a ghost from the past." He rumpled his forelock by plowing his fingers across his nearly dry hair. "Well, not exactly like Scrooge. Hogan didn't heap recriminations on my shoulders or anything like that."

"Mmm."

"I've reread the letter fifty times." He pushed back his chair and jumped to his feet. "You knew Hogan better than anyone. Why don't you read it and tell me what you think?"

He'd headed for the bedroom before Angelica could reply. The man could move like greased lightning when prompted by firecrackers, anthills or Hogan's letter. Just as quickly, he returned, plopped the letter on the table and sat in his chair.

"Read it out loud, please."

She hesitated for a moment, then removed the letter from the envelope, spread the sheet of paper on the table and began reading: " 'Dear Scutes.' "

"Stop right there. Scutes? I didn't know what the word meant until I looked it up in the dictionary. Why in the world would he call me 'scutes'?"

Angelica chuckled. She hadn't heard Hogan use the name *Rob Emery*, but she had heard him refer to Scutes. When he talked about the youngster who had reminded him so much of himself, his face would light up. Without a doubt, she knew why Hogan had left the property to his nephew: Rob was the single ray of sunshine in Hogan's family life.

"Hogan's nickname for you is a compliment. Gator scutes are like solar panels on their backside. They keep the gators' blood warm. Without them, the gators would die."

Rob leaned backward on the rear legs of his chair, not quite believing the nickname was complimentary.

Curiosity compelled Angelica to read on rather than try to convince Rob to accept the compliment graciously.

You're at the crossroads of your life. I can't explain how I know this. I just feel it in my bones. I'm hoping I'm not too late to prevent your growth from being stunted. There's something of more value than money and success in the pot of gold at the end of the rainbow. You should have a chance to be all you can be, all you ought to be. So I'm giving you an alternate path to follow. When you choose which direction you'll take, listen to your heart. It'll never lead you astray. I've treasured my memories of you.

Your loving uncle
Hogan

Slowly, Angelica folded the letter and returned it to the envelope. She wanted to keep it, to put it in the diary she'd compiled. With great reluctance she pushed the envelope toward Rob.

"Well?" His fingertips touched hers as he took the envelope and put it in his shirt pocket. "What do you think?"

"It could be just a coincidence that you received the letter in the middle of a professional crisis. He couldn't have known you were up for promotion." She shrugged. "I can't explain Hogan's sixth sense any more than Hogan himself could."

Nor *would* she explain what the letter meant, even though she knew exactly what Hogan wanted Rob to do. It was the same thing he'd made her do—examine what she held as being important and discover whether or not it was of genuine value.

"He thought my ambition to be successful 'stunted my growth,' didn't he?"

"Ambition wasn't a dirty word in Hogan's vocabulary. He had ambitions—dreams, hopes, aspirations."

"You're twisting the meaning of the word."

"Am I?" Scutes wasn't the only word Rob needed to look up in the dictionary, she mused, smiling at him. "I'd say Hogan fulfilled his ambitions."

"I'd say Hogan didn't have any ambitions to fulfill," Rob scoffed. "He never gave a damn about being successful."

Feeling her urge to defend her friend rising to the surface, where it would lead to another argument, she deliberately raised her eyebrow and took a final sip of coffee. "Let's agree to disagree on that point."

Unable to let the subject drop until he had some satisfactory answers, he said, "I wasn't speaking ill of the

dead. Hogan would be the first to tell the entire world
that being President of the United States wasn't the least
bit interesting to him.''

"I agree." Gracefully she rose to her feet, crossed to
the sink where she rinsed her cup, then added, "But if
being President of the U.S. of A. is the epitome of your
definition of ambition, then you aren't ambitious,
either, are you?''

Four

***

Rob countered, "How ambitious are you?"

He moved beside her, emptying dregs of coffee grounds from his cup into the sink. His elbow bumped hers; her forearm brushed against his waist. Touching her had the same effect on him as small puffs of air being blown on the smoldering fires of his imagination. His eyes roamed leisurely over her face, lingering on the hint of stubbornness in the line of her jaw.

She backed into the corner where the countertops joined. "I have no desire to be president, if that's what you're asking."

"Would you be interested in buying Hogan's farm?"

"No."

"I'd sell it to you at a bargain price." His eyes locked on her mouth, willing her to say yes to his offer.

She lowered her eyes to the button on his shirt to block his powers of persuasion. She wanted to help him, but letting him shift the responsibility for the gator farm from his shoulders to hers wasn't in keeping with what Hogan had intended. "I'll help you, but I won't be the escape clause in Hogan's will."

She didn't move a muscle in protest when his forefinger crooked under her chin and tilted her face upward. Tendrils of heat curled inside her as their eyes met. He wasn't a man who took refusal lightly.

"Hogan wouldn't have objected," he said softly, persuasively. "Isn't there anything I can do or say to change your mind?"

His thumb skating across her lower lip had more impact than when he'd skipped it over her knuckles while he held her hand coming back from the gator pond. Mentally she armed herself with the knowledge that his change of tactics, from hard sell to gentle persuasion, was only a disguise. Coaxing her with charm was only a means for him to reach his ultimate goal. She couldn't let him get further with sugar than he'd gotten with vinegar.

"No."

His fingers slid into her hair, unclasping the banana comb holding it at the crown of her head. She heard the plastic comb land lightly on the counter behind her as she felt his fingers thread through her hair until it spilled across her shoulders. She raised her arms to form a solid barrier between them. As though her hands had a mind of their own they settled on his chest, sliding toward the broad expanse of his shoulders.

His jade eyes darkened as the pupils expanded, inviting her to come closer. She knew what was about to happen. She wasn't naive. He was going to kiss her into submission!

"No!" she said, her voice stronger, her will weakening as he began to lower his head. Her hands tightened on the yoke of his shirt as the fragrance of mint and coffee fanned across her face.

"Those bright blue eyes of yours are contradicting you," he whispered. "Blue flames. Hot. They're saying yes ... please."

Rob wasn't certain exactly when he'd stopped thinking about the problem Hogan had bequeathed him. He only knew he couldn't ignore the beckoning rays of sunlight coming from the golden flecks in her eyes any more than a gator could turn off his scutes when the sun blazed overhead.

For one scary, heart-stopping moment he silently acknowledged his need for her warmth.

That acknowledgment made his hands drop to the counter on either side of her. Survival instincts rang alarms in his head. A man couldn't touch the sun with his bare hands without severe repercussions.

Angelica mistook his hesitation for belated pangs of conscience. Rob wouldn't stoop to using his sensual appeal on his uncle's dear friend to reach his ultimate goal of getting rid of the farm. And she wouldn't reach up and kiss him, she promised herself when her heels left the floor.

"I won't buy Hogan's property." Her voice faltered between each word.

"I'll give it to you," he murmured, fully meaning it.

"I won't take it."

She refused his generosity, but she took his kiss.

It was over in seconds. He tore his mouth free from hers as though her lips had scorched him. Shock and befuddlement tightened the skin across his high cheekbones.

Angelica felt burned around the edges, too. She knew he was a man who radiated power, strength and, on rare occasion, vulnerability. It was his taste of loneliness, confusion and desperation, combined with his quick gasp of air, that were her undoing.

She'd always been susceptible to anyone who was emotionally uneasy. She couldn't have stopped herself from returning his second kiss if her sanity had depended on it.

Desire, hot and heavy, centered inside Rob, then spiked outward. His arms circled her, raising her off her feet until she fit perfectly against him. No woman had ever responded to his tumultuous inner needs like this.

Cradled between his thighs and the cabinets, Angelica fused against him. She'd been lonely, too. Hogan's friendship had filled an emotional gap in her life, but his occasional hugs, grandfatherly pecks on the cheek and friendly pats on the shoulder had been the extent of the physical contact she'd had during the past two years. They had satisfied her human need to be touched.

Rob's kiss intensified her craving to be touched— everywhere. She arched her back until they were thigh to thigh. Her breasts flattened against the wall of his chest, aching, longing for the feel of his hands on them. Feminine needs she'd sublimated exploded as he spoke her name thickly. She threw her head back, curving her neck to accommodate the pattern of erotic kisses he peppered along her chin and throat.

Hogan's touch had satisfied a human need; Rob's touch satisfied the longings of her soul.

A screech from outside the screen door jarred through the thick haze of desire enveloping them.

"What's that clamor?" Rob muttered, lowering her so her feet were back on the floor, steadying her with his hands, then stalking toward the back porch. "Damned alligator must've gotten loose!"

"Figaro?"

Rob opened the screen door. "If it's Figaro, somebody must be standing on her tail!"

Regal as a queen attending a coronation ball, Figaro waltzed into the kitchen as though the hideous scream hadn't emerged from her bewhiskered mouth. Lithely, she jumped from the floor into Angelica's arms.

Saved by the cat, Angelica thought, burying her nose against Figaro's silky fur.

"Is that a stripe or a jealous streak running down Figaro's back?"

"A possessive streak, I'm afraid. When I moved her over to my house she had a fit until I made a second trip for her toys."

"Very un-Hogan-like. He never kept track of anything he owned."

"Did I hear a note of pleasure in that statement?"

She blinked, quite catlike, when she saw a slow smile curving his lips. The sound she heard was too rusty to be called a genuine chuckle, but it had the makings of a strong beginning.

"I wouldn't like the thought of Hogan being privy to what's going to take place between the two of us."

"Such as?" Angelica bluntly asked.

Rob leaned across the counter, placed his hands over Figaro's ears and, with equal bluntness, mouthed, "Being close, close friends. As in lovers."

She savored his response for a second before her pride had her spitting back, "A holiday fling?"

"Unlike Hogan, I can't see into the future. No sixth sense."

No common sense, either, Angelica mused, wishing he'd kept his mouth shut. Granted, she'd fervently returned his kisses, but she would have balked before entering his bedroom. Or so she told herself as she stepped around the kitchen counter. A woman who'd been perfectly content with grandfatherly affection wasn't the type to be overwhelmed by a man making a pass at her.

He'd been frank with her; she'd return the favor. "What about love and commitment?"

"I'm not ruling them out," he responded glibly. "After I get rid of the gator farm, I'd enjoy showing you the bright lights of New York City."

Angelica shook her head. Hogan had given her a home to get her away from the bright lights and the demands of city living. How mistaken Rob was to dangle them in front of her like a strand of Christmas lights.

"No, thanks." To take the sting out of her rejection, she added, "But I'm flattered by your offer."

Moments later, Rob stood on the back porch watching Angelica skirt through the palmettos. Her erect posture was duplicated by Hogan's cat. Tail held high, Figaro followed her without a backward glance.

He'd wanted to argue with her, to make her stay until she threw the cat outside and walked back into his arms. But aside from stopping her with another body block, he knew there was nothing he could do.

He'd never experienced somebody walking serenely away from him. And she'd repeatedly refused his generosity. He'd offered to sell her the farm, then to give it to her. He'd offered to take her with him when he returned to New York. He'd never offered a woman so much, and been so firmly rebuffed.

She'd been flattered; he'd been devastated.

All right, Emery, get hold of your bootstraps and pull yourself out of here. She doesn't want you on your terms—hell, on any terms. You're losing your touch, fella, both at work and with women.

Since he'd gone into advertising, he'd had the Midas touch. Every project he'd undertaken had turned into a pot of gold for his clients. He wasn't a billionaire, but at least he had a microwave oven and a toaster, which was more than he could say for his uncle's ill-equipped kitchen!

Egotistically, he wondered what his uncle had that he didn't? Youth? No! Vitality? No! Success? No! The odds should have been stacked in his favor. Angelica should have welcomed him with open arms.

His thoughts turned as green with jealousy as his eyes. Last night, she'd said Hogan was her friend. Rob had hesitated at leaping to the conclusion of their being the Hollywood version for "friends."

Nah, he thought, shaking his head. He felt fairly certain Angelica hadn't been his uncle's mistress. If she had been financially tied to his uncle, she'd have jumped at Rob's offers.

What the heck, he hadn't come to Florida looking for a beautiful woman to share his vacation. He didn't need her or her helping hands. She could have been a pleasant diversion from an unpleasant duty, but he didn't need her. If she chose to bury herself in this godforsaken swamp, that was her problem.

The taste of sour grapes made his throat work overtime. He circled his stomach with the flat of his hand. A familiar burning sensation that ignited when he was thoroughly stymied and frustrated was gnawing savagely at his insides. He'd had his yearly medical checkup and had walked away with a clean bill of health, but he suspected he was a prime candidate for ulcers.

"The fact remains—she rejected me. Accept it." He caught his last glimpse of Angelica as she climbed the steps to her front porch and disappeared into the house. Pondering all the facts, he added, "Okay, also accept the fact that you can't change what's taken place in her past, either. She must have loved Hogan. Accepting those premises, what you have to do is go on from there!"

Where? How? How in the blazes was he supposed to compete with a ghost for Angelica's affection? At that moment, he'd have given up his costly apartment on Manhattan Island for the tiniest clue to solving his problem.

Persistence, he mused, that's the missing factor in solving the problem.

He'd made a mistake by letting her abruptly end the discussion. He should have detained her or he should have followed her. Not being a man who gave up by doing nothing to correct a strategic mistake, Rob strode to the cupboard over the sink.

She'd refused his advances, but she'd never refuse a neighbor who needed a cup of sugar, would she? An old ploy, Rob knew, but one that seldom failed to work. If she was out of sugar, he could always ask for those books she'd promised to lend him.

Feeling better once he'd decided what action to take, he set out, letting the screen door slam behind him. His self-defeating thoughts were behind him, too. The more he considered the situation the more certain he felt that stick-to-itiveness was what glued his world together.

* * *

"Figaro, stop being a nuisance," Angelica chided,

gently nudging the cat aside with her foot to break the figure eight Figaro was making between her feet. "You can curl up on my lap while I'm working, after I'm finished putting the soup together. You're getting to be a lazy lap cat, or a slave driver—I don't know which."

The rumble of Figaro's purr as she made a final swipe against Angelica's leg didn't provide a decipherable answer. The cat sat back on her haunches. "Meow-rrrr."

"Very pathetic. Nice try, but it won't get me to fix seafood chowder for you. I know you don't like chicken soup, but this isn't for you. Scat!"

Angelica selected the French knife from the butcher's block and made quick work of dicing the carrots and celery. Seasoned chicken stock simmered on the stove permeating the air with the fragrance of fresh herbs.

"He probably hasn't had a decent bowl of soup since he left his mother's home. I bet he eats nothing but fast food. That's what makes him grouchy, not to mention his caffeine addiction and a habit of skipping breakfast."

She glanced down. Figaro was busy, grooming her front paws with her pink tongue, and ignoring the chatter.

"That's right. You have to take care of yourself and so does he." Feeling a tiny bit guilty for increasing Rob's stress level, she'd decided to make amends by delivering a pot of soup to his doorstep. She justified her altruistic behavior to Figaro by adding, "Hogan would have wanted the three of us to get along."

She'd shoved a relaxation tape into the tape recorder the instant she walked into the house and had spent a minute or two with her eyes closed, imagining she was lying on a quiet beach. That had taken the edge off her own frustration.

Stress busters, she mused, pausing to listen to the reproduced sounds of the ocean washing over the shore. Volumes had been published on how to relieve stress, but she'd bet a nickel to a doughnut hole that Rob hadn't read one of them. There was little doubt in her mind that the psychiatrist who'd be interviewing him would detect how close the man was to total burnout. Without benefit of testing or prolonged interviews, she'd recognized his symptoms: forgetfulness, irritability, tenseness.

"Two weeks," she murmured, picking up the cutting board and crossing to the stove. She raked the vegetables into the pot. "Time enough to take a kindly dose of stress-buster medicine."

A selfish thought entered her mind. What would happen if he returned to New York with his nerves frayed from the additional tension caused by the gator farm? If he didn't sell the farm and wasn't promoted...and he had a reason to move south... *me*...maybe...

She dismissed the unworthy thought with a swirl of the spoon in the chicken broth. She advocated a balanced life-style to her patients: work, play and love intertwined. The kind of love she wanted, deep abiding love, couldn't survive if rooted in dissatisfaction or failure. Love could only thrive and grow when both partners were allowed to reach their utmost potential. She told this to her clients because she believed it herself.

She'd offered to help Rob. Whether he wanted it or not, that was exactly what she planned on doing. Chicken soup was only the beginning.

Rob knocked on her screen door as he called, "Angelica?"

"Think of the devil and he pops up on your front porch," she muttered to Figaro, grinning. Then she shouted, "Come on in. I'm in the kitchen."

Figaro bounded toward the living room and Angelica followed. Her grin widened when she observed Rob stooping to pet Figaro. An empty cup dangled from his forefinger.

"You must have inhaled that pot of coffee," she teased lightly.

"Uh-uh." He jackknifed to his feet, holding Figaro against his chest. "I'm out of sugar."

"You're going to bake something?" She couldn't keep the skepticism out of her voice. Some men were handy in the kitchen, but she doubted Rob took the time from his work schedule to boil a hot dog. Her heart fluttered when he genuinely smiled and handed her the cup.

"Sounds like a female chauvinist remark to me. What do you think, Figaro? Is she implying a man can't bake a batch of cookies?"

Figaro's purring increased to the volume of a local freight train.

"No chauvinism intended." She turned toward the kitchen. "I hope you plan on sharing what you bake. I'm fixing soup for your lunch."

Sniffing the air, Rob felt his mouth begin to water. "Chicken noodle?"

"Chicken and homemade stuffed noodles." She removed the lid from the sugar canister. "Will one cup of sugar be enough?"

Following her into the kitchen, his eyes dropped to the sway of her tight derriere, down the length of her slender legs. They bounced up to a respectful level when she pivoted on one foot. He hadn't the vaguest idea how much sugar it took to make a batch of cookies.

"It'll do." Should have stuck to the I've-come-to-borrow-those-books-you-promised excuse, he thought, wondering if the small town he'd driven through last night had a bakery.

"What kind are you going to fix?"

"Chocolate chip." He wanted to allow for the possibility of there not being a bakery in town, so he picked what he hoped would be the easiest to prepare. Little kids fixed chocolate chip cookies, didn't they? He could do it. Anybody who could read could follow a recipe. "They're my favorite."

"You'll need a cookie sheet, tinfoil and a large mixing bowl, too." Heart racing, she hunkered down to the bottom row of cabinets, then made the mistake of glancing up at him. His fingers gently massaged beneath Figaro's ear, the cat's favorite place to be stroked. She absolutely, positively would not volunteer to make the cookies for him, despite that engaging grin still plastered on his face. "Cooking utensils are in short supply at your place."

Finding an easy out and grabbing it, Rob rolled his tongue in the side of his cheek and said, "This is too much trouble for you. I'll buy some cookies while I'm in Oviedo talking to the realtor."

His engaging smile had a crooked tilt that reminded her of a boy caught with his hand in the cookie jar. He had no more planned on baking cookies than the man in the moon baked moon pies. She rose, chuckling at the irony of a brilliant advertising man reduced to using such an old line.

"You don't have to borrow sugar to be welcome over here. After all, you are my landlord. Which reminds me..." She crooked her finger for him to follow her. She walked to a side door and opened it, then stood aside, motioning for him to precede her. "You'll be wanting Hogan's plants, too."

"Orchids?" Rob knew less about raising exotic flowers than he knew about alligators. Sure, he recognized the purple kind that he'd given his date to the prom, but that was the sum total of his experience with orchids. He raised his thumb toward her for her inspection. "I have a black thumb."

"These are easy growers." She slipped by him, pointing upward to the various pots hanging from the rafters. She refrained from touching the blooms; they bruised easily. As she walked down the length of the greenhouse she recited pertinent facts about each species. "*Phalaenopsis*—white, pink and yellow—commonly known as moth orchids. *Paphiopedilum*, the lady's slipper, yellow, green, mahogany. Hogan preferred the speckled varieties. Miniature cymbidiums, white and yellow with tones of red and green. Cattleya, that's the one the florists use most often. They're a bit tougher to grow, but I'll help you with them."

Groaning, Rob asked, "What am I going to do with hothouse flowers in New York?"

"Enjoy them," Angelica suggested wryly. "It's a rewarding hobby."

He'd learned that her definition of rewarding had nothing to do with money. "How?"

"Tension tamers."

Rob held out one hand; it quivered. "Tension makers."

"Initially, perhaps. But—"

"No buts about this." His smile had sagged into a straight line. "Orchids and ol' Arnold down at the pond are tension makers! There isn't anything else my dear departed uncle left me that I should know about, is there?"

"Figaro was Hogan's cat. I suppose..."

Rob straightened the arm where the cat had snuggled against him. Figaro dug her front claws into Rob's shirtfront.

"Here." He disregarded the cat's startled mewing and adroitly peeled her claws off his shirt. "She's your cat."

"Come on, Fig, the man apparently doesn't know a good thing when it's right there in his arms," she mumbled, turning her back on Rob and reentering the house. He'd rejected the gators, the orchids and the cat, she fumed. Everything Hogan loved, Rob considered a stress builder. It was a good thing she wasn't one of Hogan's belongings, or he'd reject her, too! In a voice loud enough for Rob to hear, she said, "Next he'll be trying to convince us that stroking you didn't soothe him more than it did you! We can't help him if he won't help himself!"

"Something tells me I'll be eating lunch at a burger joint," Rob grumbled to himself, wondering how it would be physically possible to walk back into the kitchen with his foot in his mouth.

He should have taken the damned orchids and eaten them for lunch! But no, he'd wanted to do the right thing by letting her keep them. But before he could offer them to her, she'd offered to help him take care of them. Couldn't the woman graciously accept a gift? Did she always have to be the giver and never be on the receiving end? Other women would have been delighted to receive a hothouse full of orchids; they'd have taken the gesture as a sign of undying love, for crying out loud!

Angelica suppressed the urge to pack her bags and get off Rob's property before he considered her one of his stress builders. She dropped Figaro onto her favorite chair, then crossed to the stove, where she stirred the soup vigorously. The remembrance of Rob's winning smile, of what he could be if he weren't so darned uptight, kept her feet rooted to Hogan's floor.

Patience, she told herself as she seethed. She had to take charge of her anger. She wouldn't allow herself to dwell on what she'd like to tell him. She had to zero in on how she felt, get in touch with her own emotions. Giving Rob the international high sign as she stalked out the door with her suitcase wouldn't make him feel apologetic or cooperative.

Anger was self-defeating.

She dropped the spoon in the ladle dish, snatched a pad off the counter and began writing. Anger poured through her pen. By writing down her frustrations she'd be clearing the air of the smoke and fumes of her anger.

He doesn't know what's good for him, she wrote, punctuating the statement with an exclamation point. His values are screwed up! He's too damned independent and self-sufficient to accept help, even when he desperately needs it!

She paused, waiting for her perspective to be restored. Awareness, understanding and then action were the three keys that unlocked frustration. She needed all of them.

She read what she'd written. She asked herself if what she'd written were important issues. They were! But she knew her anger would only get in the way of solving the problems.

She ripped the page off the pad. Methodically, she began tearing the sheet of paper into minuscule pieces. She strode to the trash can and let the pieces of paper filter through her fingers.

Instantly, she felt an emotional release. The symbolic action, combined with the physical and mental energy spent in performing it, relieved her of the burden of her anger. She'd effectively defused her explosive temper. She closed her eyes, trying to see Rob as Hogan must have seen him, with a brilliant white love light surrounding him.

Silently, Rob stood in the doorway watching her while she flicked the last piece of confetti off her smallest finger. Eyes squeezed shut, her face gradually lost its flush and regained its normal golden tan. Her clenched jaw relaxed.

Still feeling the knife points of his frustration, he asked, "How did you do that? Switch from hotter than hell's fires to complete tranquillity."

"I wrote it out, then destroyed it. There are other ways, but the pad was handy."

He glanced into the waste can, wondering what she'd written, and yet not really wanting to know. He took the pad and pencil when she handed them to him. He wasn't a lamebrained idiot; he knew what to do.

In his distinct scrawl, he began writing: Angelica is a giver, never takes. She tosses my generosity back in my face. She's too damned self-sufficient! And too damned appealing for her own good!

The pencil lead broke.

"Okay," Angelica said in the calming voice she used with her clients. "Now ask yourself . . . how important is what I've written down?"

"I think they are important."

"Fine. Will your anger change any of them?"

Rob shook his head. Slowly, he began shredding the sheet.

"You've spilled your anger on that paper and you're destroying it. You could burn it, or stomp on it, or flush it down the toilet, but the minute the paper leaves your hand, close your eyes and visualize your anger leaving you, too. Don't hold on to it. Let it go."

Eyes shut, Rob let the bits and pieces dribble through his fingers. He didn't know if it had been her gimmick or her hypnotic voice that had done the trick, but the burning sensation in his stomach began to subside. He opened his eyes and stared at Angelica. "It worked."

"Surprised?"

"Frankly? Yes. But I'm surprised you, of all people, would need a means to cope with anger. You're almost as laid-back as my uncle."

Angelica grinned at what she considered a compliment. "Before I met Hogan, there were days when my pent-up anger had my insides boiling with rage. Mount St. Helens was like a small-town Fourth of July picnic compared to some of the tantrums I wanted to throw."

"I'm in touch with that." He rubbed the flat of his palm across his waist, then automatically glanced at his Rolex watch. "Sometimes my stomach rolls faster than a commercial running on fast forward."

"Push the slow motion button. Get rid of your watch."

Although her suggestion had appeal, it also appalled him. "Without my watch, I'd be perpetually late. That really gets the gastric juices rumbling."

"What's the worst thing that could happen if you were occasionally late?"

"Are you kidding? I'd be fired in a New York minute!" He snapped his fingers for emphasis.

"Your job depends on punctuality," Angelica said calmly, letting him know she'd heard him, but wasn't buying what he'd said. "You're probably one of those executive types who usually arrives early for appointments."

"I am."

"And while you're waiting for the other person to arrive, you're either pencil-tapping or you have a white-knuckle grip on the closest inanimate object—like a telephone or steering wheel. Right?"

Rob shifted restlessly. "The center drawer of my desk is a graveyard for broken pencils," he admitted reluctantly.

"By the time the other person gets there, the muscles in the back of your neck straight down your spine are bunched into knots." She propped her elbows on the counter and leaned toward him. "Isn't that counterproductive?"

"Probably. I guess you think I should keep a pad of paper, a ballpoint pen and a trash can handy at all times." A small smile tugged at the corners of his mouth.

"That's a starting point. But my guess is that anger and frustration are only symptomatic of the root problem. You might want to consider what you're holding on to when you snap one of your pencils in half."

She wanted him to make the connection between his desire to control time and the time bomb ticking away inside his stomach. If he were her patient, she'd be counseling him for the next few months. She'd have slowly guided him toward the cause of his habit of breaking pencils. Unfortunately, she couldn't control time any more than Rob could.

Rob narrowed his eyes as he listened to her. Something about her didn't mesh with his first assessment—that she was the star of a modern-day version of the old film *Tammy and the Bachelor*. Much as the story line of a naive backwoods girl being saved from total ignorance by a suave hero appealed to him, his gut instincts told him Angelica wasn't a Tammy.

How had Angelica learned about coping with anger? Fear of tardiness? Muscles bunching with tension? She sounded as though she'd had firsthand experience with what she'd called "white-knuckle" intensity. Raising gator eggs and orchids wouldn't put her under that kind of stress.

What had?

There was a missing link between the laid-back lifestyle he'd observed and the ease with which she dispensed tips on how he could learn to control his temper. Had Hogan and his sixth sense influenced her life? Was Hogan the missing link?

"Gators, orchids and pop psychology, here in the swamps of Florida? Just exactly where were you when you met Hogan?"

"Orlando," Angelica replied succinctly as she braced her arms and pushed away from the counter. Tell him you're a psychiatrist, her superego prodded. He hates shrinks, her pleasure-oriented id countered. Blab, and he'll be out of here, in one of his New York minutes!

Her ego filtered the messages, searching for an ideal solution. "At the hospital."

"You're a nurse?"

"No."

"A doctor?" He stepped around the corner of the counter and moved in on her when her head bobbed up and down. She's a doctor! What kind of doctor? Why are her eyes avoiding me? What's she hiding? "A geriatric doctor?"

"No." She pasted a high-voltage smile on her face to detract from what she had to tell him. "I'm a psychiatrist."

Five

Rob grabbed the pencil he'd used and scribbled, "Shrink!"

Without bothering to shred the page to rid himself of his anger, he broke the pencil in half, tossed it on the pad and stormed from her kitchen through the living room.

Figaro added insult to injury by jumping off her chair and tagging along after him. Nose in the air, tail bristled like a bottle brush, she barely made it through the door before it slammed shut.

Angelica turned the pad around. Using the stub of the pencil she wrote, "Better a shrink than a parasite living off your uncle!"

Unwilling to let her anger eat at her equilibrium, she wadded the page and threw it against the wall. Dissatisfied by the lack of noise the wad made as it hit the wall, she strode over to it and placed her foot squarely on it. As her foot rotated in a circular motion, flattening the wad into a crinkled mass, she gritted, "Let it go. That isn't important to you! Forget it."

Her anger gradually dissipated with each twist of her ankle, but she knew she'd been deluding herself if she denied that Rob's instant reaction had hurt. Considering the fact that his promotion depended upon a psychological profile compiled by a New York psychiatrist, she could understand why he felt threatened by her occupation.

"The man is obsessed with career advancement," she mumbled, wishing Figaro hadn't absconded with Rob. Holding the cat would have given her tactile pleasure. She doubted Rob would benefit from Figaro's presence.

"Appreciating Figaro is only one of our minor differences."

She picked up the piece of paper and dropped it into the trash can. Crossing to the stove, she slowly circled the ladle in the simmering broth. As she did so, she dug deeper into her psyche to find the basis of the sore points between them. He thought the ultimate joy in life was winning an award for the best commercial of the year; she pushed the mute button on the television's remote control when the commercials interrupted her program. He believed the simple pleasures in life were a waste of time; she thought his time-motion studies were a waste of time and paper. He vented his frustrations on pencils; she shredded paper.

None of the differences she mentally tabulated was the real bone of contention. She had to look further.

"What he thinks is worthless, I hold dear. What he thinks is of utmost importance, I know from personal experience has little value."

But how could she convince him that his goal of becoming vice president of an advertising agency wouldn't bring him happiness? There would always be another rung on the corporate ladder beyond his reach. He'd work harder and harder, until he physically collapsed or finally realized his self-esteem wasn't climbing an inch higher than it had been the day he painted watercolor pictures with Hogan. She'd never be able to convince him that Hogan's sixth sense had been accurate: Rob Emery's emotional growth had been stunted by ambition.

His viewpoint wouldn't change; hers wouldn't, either.

Steam from the soup reminded her of one viewpoint they shared: physical attraction. When she looked into those tropical green eyes of his, her id went crazy. Sparks flew. Her heart thudded like the bass drum of a rock group.

Maybe she should listen to her id when it shouted, "Gimme, gimme, gimme!"

What was wrong with having sex with an attractive, intelligent man? She wasn't a virgin, for heaven's sake. Curiosity about the normal sex drive of the human body and the corresponding emotional highs her roommates had extolled had led her into sharing a bed with a handsome medical student.

Her eyes tilted upward as she remembered that experience. Silently, she chuckled. She'd been too intense, too clinical, too...inexperienced. Their encounter had been heavily sprinkled with "sorry" and "excuse me." She'd left the motel room wondering if they'd both sprouted extra sets of elbows, knees and noses. He hadn't asked for a repeat performance; she wouldn't have indulged in sex with him again if she had been invited.

Her curiosity had been satisfied, completely, until her friends began issuing wedding invitations. Peer pressure applied on the jugular vein, she mused. She'd been in residence at Faith Memorial by then, dating an intern. Her parents thought she'd met the ideal man. He and she had similar backgrounds, interests and goals. Everyone looked at them as the perfect couple. Bells in church steeples should have been ringing as they passed by on their way to his apartment.

Rationally, she'd been certain they'd "click"—that was what her married friends said would happen—in bed. This time, it would be different. Better. Or so she'd promised herself.

She knew what to expect. She'd read every how-to-do-it book in the medical library, in case doing what came naturally didn't, for her.

Peculiar thing about friendship, she thought. It didn't automatically blossom into heart-stopping passion, regardless of how it had been nurtured. At best, she'd walked away from the intern's apartment thinking of sex as...pleasant.

And yet, some undefinable emotion she hadn't yet experienced had been kindled deep within her when Rob suggested having a holiday fling with her. Uneasy with her physical reaction to him, she'd doused the tiny flames darting between them by inquiring about love and commitment. Just as he must have known it was presumptuous to invite her into his bedroom on such short acquaintance, she'd known it was too soon to expect an avowal of undying love from him.

"On such short acquaintance...too soon..." Angelica repeated her thoughts aloud, twice. Both phrases were time qualifiers. To her chagrin, she realized she was guilty of doing exactly what she'd diagnosed as the major cause of Rob's stress: wasting energy trying to control time—especially future time.

He held on to every precious moment with white-knuckle intensity to make certain he'd packed his hours of the day with worthwhile activities. In effect, she'd been pointing to the days on the calendar and saying, "We haven't had time to get to know each other."

She'd tried to control the future by putting stipulations on the here and now!

She dropped the spoon into the sink and hurried to her desk to search for Hogan's exact thoughts on time management. While he was in the hospital, they'd argued about time being of the essence. She paged through her diary now until she found the place.

Here it is, she thought, reading aloud. "Time and a gator's breath have a couple of things in common—you can't see them, and you sure can't hold on to them! Who in their right mind would want to?" Her finger slid down the page. "Yesterdays and tomorrows exist only in man's mind. Animals are smarter than humans." She grinned at the last question he'd posed. "Do you think God created the minute hand on watches? He only gave us the sun to show us what time to get up and what time to start getting ready for bed."

Armed with Hogan's wisdom and her self-realizations, she placed the diary back in the desk. Attitudes about time can be changed if a person is willing, she thought, feeling composed. She'd changed. Maybe Rob could, too.

"If he's willing..." she said aloud. "*Only* if he's willing."

Parked between the two cabins, Rob folded his arms across the rim of the steering wheel and stared at Angelica's front door. He'd had a busy morning. The main street of the small town had been bustling with activity. A bizarre mix of rural folks from the agricultural area surrounding the town and yuppies from the planned community of Tuskawilla mingled on the sidewalks.

Rob's first stop had been at the realtor's office. The agent had told him the alligator farm could be sold for a handsome profit...eventually. He would contact a few speculators to see if any of them would be interested in developing the land. When Rob tried to pin him down on how long it would take, the man had become increasingly vague. Rob had walked out of the office, without listing the property.

On the way back to his car, he'd passed a red-and-white-striped pole. He'd paused, cupped his hands beside his face to block the sun from turning the window into a mirror and peered into the barbershop. He'd wondered if it was really true that a barbershop was the small-town version of the men's executive bathroom in a major corporation. Impulsively, he'd decided to go in for a trim and find out.

Politely ignored by the men in the shop, he'd waited for his turn in the barber's chair. From behind an opened newspaper, he'd avidly listened to the exchange of local gossip. So-and-so's wife had had her baby, a strapping ten-pounder. The Conklin girl was getting married to Bud's oldest son the first week in June. Pete somebody or other had bought a brand-new pickup truck.

Rob had almost given up on hearing local news of interest to him when the man seated next to him announced he'd recently closed the deal on his citrus farm. Within seconds, Rob folded his paper and spoke up. All eyes turned on him when he mentioned Hogan's name.

Several men introduced themselves as though they were long-lost relatives when he told them he was Hogan's nephew.

During the next hour, he got his hair trimmed shorter than he preferred, but he also got an earful about Hogan and Angelica. He strode out into the bright noon sun somewhat baffled by the townspeople's opinion of Hogan Potter, the local philanthropist who slipped money into the pockets of those needing it while on his way to various senior citizen's homes with bouquets of orchids, and Angelica Franklin, earthbound angel who worked miracles with families in trouble!

He'd left the barbershop and wandered down Broadway in a daze. His Uncle Hogan was a local hero? And Angelica was a heroine? That was a far cry from Hogan the footloose vagabond and Angelica the shrink!

How could he have been so utterly wrong about both of them? He inwardly shuddered when he remembered implying Angelica had lived off his uncle's generosity. No wonder she'd constantly refused his misplaced generosity. She should have slapped him!

But what had she done? She'd blithely offered to help him. It was part of her job to help people.

No, he corrected, smoothing his brow with his fingers. Her helping people was more than her job. It was who and what she was. Kind. Generous. Trustworthy.

He'd found himself standing in front of a florist's shop as he contemplated the errors in judgment he'd made. There wasn't a means for him to tell Hogan he'd been mistaken, but he could try to make amends to Angelica.

Apologies weren't easy for him. He'd lived too many years making intuitive decisions, plunging full speed ahead and damning the consequences. Until now, he'd

felt as though he had a fairly clean record, one devoid
of any horrendous blunders. Minor bungles with
women had been rectified by having Olivia send a dozen
roses to the lady he'd offended.

He'd stared at the display of flowers in the florist's
window, realizing how ridiculous it would be to buy
roses for a lady who raised orchids. The array of flowers
she'd been watering in her backyard could stock a New
York florist's showroom!

He'd spent the next two hours searching for something as unique as the person he was buying it for.

Now Rob turned his head toward the package on the
passenger's seat of the car. Never in his life had he paid
his hard-earned money for anything so whimsical.
When she unwrapped it, she would think he'd gone
completely around the bend.

"What the hell," he muttered as he opened the door
with one hand and picked up the oddly shaped package with the other. "I can't make a bigger fool of myself than I already have."

Angelica heard his footsteps on the wooden treads of
the porch. Glad he'd returned without her having had
to seek him out, she raced to the front door. What she
saw when she opened the door made her heart thud
joyfully in her chest. Hair shorn unfashionably short by
New York standards, an abashed grin on his face and
holding a gaily wrapped package she felt certain was
meant for her, he was as appealing as an ice-cold slice
of watermelon on a hot day in August.

Wordlessly, he handed her the present. For a man
who prided himself on original clever phrases, he was
completely tongue-tied. All he could think of was how
gorgeous she looked in her pink jumpsuit, with her
honey-blond hair hanging loose on her shoulders, and

what a miserable piece of gator dung he was for not be-
lieving his eyes the first time he'd seen her. She positively radiated goodness.

"Come in! The soup is ready." Angelica juggled the
bulky package from one arm to the other as she ran her
fingers over it, trying to guess what was beneath the
wrapping paper. She squeezed, sniffed, then giggled
girlishly in pure delight. "It's squeezable. A pillow?"

Rob shook his head.

"Can't be chocolates. They would be in a box and I'd
smell them." Peeking between gaps in the paper, unable to contain her curiosity a moment longer, she
pushed aside the bright yellow ribbon bow and peeled
off the paper. A pink satin flamingo with outrageously
long curly orange eyelashes popped from the paper.
Angelica gasped in pleasure. Hugging her gift, she
twirled around in a small circle and said, "What a terrific gift! I love it! Thank you, thank you, thank you!"

The next thing Rob knew, she'd hugged him and
painted a pale pink imprint of her lips on his cheek.

"I'm s-s-sorry about the way I've behaved," tumbled from his mouth.

"Apology accepted." She clasped the jaunty flamingo in a one-armed bear hug and put her empty hand
in the crook of Rob's arm. "I don't know about you,
but I'm starving. I hope you didn't eat lunch while you
were in town."

"Only a king-size wedge of humble pie served at the
barbershop," he admitted, amazed by the power of a
simple apology and a wacky gift. "You've earned quite
a reputation."

"Mmm?" She put the flamingo on the windowsill in
the dinette where she could admire it as she ladled soup
into the bowls.

"Where do you keep your wings and halo?" he teased, feeling as though he'd climbed from the depths of a dark hole straight to the top of the world as he seated himself at the table.

Angelica chuckled, dipping into the soup pot and giving him an extra fat stuffed noodle. "Don't believe everything you hear. Those same people who sang my praises today are probably kin to the ones who thought I was some sort of hocus-pocus witch doctor when I first opened my office. *Real* doctors are supposed to come equipped with little black medical bags filled with stethoscopes and modern medicines."

"You arrived with only a couch?"

"Uh-uh. No couch. Most of my patients at the hospital felt uncomfortable flat on their backs with me sitting in a chair hovering over them. My office is almost a duplicate of my living room—give or take a few knickknacks."

He spread his napkin on his lap as she served the soup.

"Hot tea or iced tea?"

"Does the hot tea come with tea leaves for you to read?" he asked, poker-faced. Only the sparkle in his eyes indicated he was joking with her. "I'm becoming a devout believer in hocus-pocus."

"A convert!" Angelica replied in mock wonder, clapping her hands over her heart. "Ooh, you're gonna love my tea leaf tricks. I'll toss a mint leaf in your cup to spice up the reading."

"I can hardly wait."

"Don't. Go ahead and dig in to your soup while I put the kettle on to boil."

Rob didn't make polite refusals. The aroma of chicken and herbs was too much to resist. His taste buds merrily celebrated the truce between him and Angelica when the broth touched them. "Soup's delicious."

You're delicious, he silently added, watching a mischievous smile dancing at the corners of her mouth while she filled the teapot.

Angelica's imagination ran rampant as she thought of titillating tidbits to tell as she gazed at the tea leaves. It was the perfect opportunity for her to convey a fanciful list of things he could be doing to eliminate stress. Of course, when she visualized him hugging and stroking someone, that person would just happen to fit her description.

"I've decided not to sell the farm," Rob said, breaking into her reverie.

"Oh yeah? What are you going to do with it?" She crossed her fingers and sent a quick prayer in Hogan's direction.

"With your help, I'll run it for the next two weeks. Who knows? The word is out in town. Maybe someone will turn up who'll take over the operation."

"And if they don't?"

She eased into the chair across from him. Her toes and knees bumped against his. Their eyes collided. He didn't move; she didn't move, either, not until his feet moved to the outside of her feet.

"We'll have to look into the possibilities of releasing the gators. It's still what I'd prefer to do. The only offer I had at the barbershop was a man who said he'd slaughter them." He brushed his lips with his napkin. "I know I can't tear down the fence and herd them toward the river. In the back of my mind, I keep remembering a movie Hogan took me to see when I was a kid. *Born Free*. Remember it?"

"Yeah, and I bawled my eyes out when I read the books and found out the lion died." His wanting to free the gators had a similar effect. The soup she swallowed had a distinctly salty flavor.

Clearing her throat she pointed the handle of her spoon at him. "One thing you have to keep in mind is the difference between alligators and lions, along with the differences in their habitat. This piece of property isn't in the middle of a game preserve in Africa."

Rob downed the last swig of his tea. He passed the cup to her. With a cocky grin, he said, "Tell me what you see in my future."

"One mint leaf and several soggy tea leaves."

"C'mon, Dr. Hocus Pocus," he chided. "You can do better than that. Take another look."

Angelica chuckled. She waved her fingers in a circular motion over the lip of the cup. Eyelashes fluttering to narrow slits, she began droning. A shiver raced from her knees to her heart when his knees constricted against hers. With the same melodic tones she practiced when hypnotizing a client, she murmured, "I see a woman reaching out to you."

"Tall, dark and handsome?"

She raised one eyelid. Her blue eye twinkled with mischief. "Nope. Have you been sneaking a peek at my tea leaves?"

"Uh-uh. Do you think you could give me a description of my woman?"

Brashly, she replied, "Blond. Blue eyes. About my height."

Through her fringe of lashes she watched for his reaction. When his smile stretched to wider dimensions, her heart expanded until it felt twice its size.

"Intriguing," Rob whispered, not wanting to break her magical spell. "Do you see the standard ocean voyage?"

"Travel? Ah yes, I see a trip." Her fingers raised. "What's this? Have you been experiencing forgetfulness? Flights of fantasy? Are you too tired to lift a finger, but constantly feeling pushed to climb to new heights?"

"Yes."

She swirled the cup. "I see you writing something. You're cutting the paper into strips and putting them in a cookie jar."

"What did I write?"

"Let me see." She lifted the cup upward. "'I can be everything I want to be' is on one slip. On another slip, I see your name with vice president written beside it."

"Any bad stuff in my cookie jar?"

"No. Only fabulous things you've accomplished and things you fervently hope to gain." A positive-thinking list cut into strips, she added silently. "When you're feeling down, you reach into your cookie jar for a treat."

She shushed him when he started to comment. Remembering what he'd told her about his uncle's teaching him the rudiments of watercolor painting, she said, "I'm getting another insight. Swirls of pastels. Pale blue...peaceful. Vibrant pink and yellows. Cool greens. You're...painting?"

Taking another peek, she watched him leaning closer and closer to her. He removed the cup from her hands.

He peered into the cup. Imitating her soothing voice, he said, "I see water. Waves."

"Rob, I didn't see a sea voyage."

"Shh! I'm not on a ship. I'm stretched out on a sandy beach. Turquoise water is breaking over— Wait a minute. The woman you saw? She's stretched out beside me."

"Oh, yeah? Is she wearing a one-piece, purple bathing suit that has rows of pink, white and turquoise blue ruffles along the V neckline?"

"You are peeking! That's a perfect description. Wonder who it could be?"

Angelica laughed. "Can't be me. I have a two-piece. Lime green, with a matching cover-up..."

"I see her. She's the one dribbling suntan oil on my back! She's whispering in my ear." He held the cup closer to his ear. "I think she's telling me other techniques to ease the tension in my life."

His feet rubbed against hers. He placed the cup back on the table. He lifted her hand to his lips. "Could I tempt you into a trip to Cocoa Beach?"

"Now?"

"This instant."

She couldn't refuse, not after the pep talk she'd given herself about time, living every moment to the fullest.

"Yeah. I'd like that."

"Great!" He bounced to his feet before she could have second thoughts. "Get your beach bag while I dig my trunks out of the suitcase. I'll meet you at the car."

Neither of them wore a watch, but the sun had traveled an hour's distance when Rob spread their beach towels on the sand. On the short trip to the Atlantic coast, he'd been the complete opposite of the man who'd arrived in the middle of the night. Carefree, he'd sung along with the radio. If he didn't know the words, he made them up as he went along.

This was a side of his personality Angelica hadn't seen previously. She'd been drawn to him. Long before they turned onto the road that led to the beach, she'd scooted next to him, put her arm across his shoulder and tried to harmonize with him.

Rob sucked the ocean's breeze into his lungs. He felt good. Damned good, he mused, revitalized, charged with energy. He knew how Tarzan must have felt when he pounded on his chest and bellowed with exuberance.

"C'mon! Last one in has to feed the gators tomorrow!" Angelica shouted over her shoulder, racing toward the water's edge.

Always ready to take on a new challenge, Rob dug his toes into the hot sand and sprinted after her. As he passed her, he looped his arm around her waist, carrying her with him. Knees churning, they hopped the shallow waves until they were waist deep in the ocean. Letting go of her, Rob swiped at the surface of the water.

"You're asking for it," Angelica threatened, wiping the saltwater off her face. "Splash me again and you'll be dribbling suntan oil on your own back."

"I'd rather do the dribbling on your back." The wind tossed her hair, highlighting the silky strands with sunshine. His skin warmed under the brightness of her smile. In two strides he was next to her. "You must have been a lovely sea creature in some past life. A mermaid who beckoned unwary sailors into the briny deep with a siren's song."

Without a second thought, her fingers trekked up his chest to the hollows of his collarbone. Drops of water clung to her eyelashes, acting as prisms of light, haloing him in rainbow shades of violet, green and blue. "Would you jump into water over your head for me?"

"Mmm-hmm." His arms circled her waist. "As long as you promise to resuscitate me with the kiss of life. I swear, lady, I'm drowning in your eyes at this very moment."

At this very moment, she silently repeated, floating against him. She wouldn't grab for the future; she'd vowed to be content with the present. She'd keep her vow.

Shoulder deep in water, Rob turned to block the force of the rolling waves. His feet were spread to maintain his balance. She bobbed against him as he gently lifted her until their eyes met. Deep green jungle fires burned in the depths of his eyes. He tested the pliancy of her lips with his forefinger.

Her lips parted, eager for him. Her arms twined around his neck. Did her eyes close because of the blinding sun or because the brilliant flashes of hot desire she read in Rob's eyes blinded her to any warning her tormented mind might have sent.

He shifted again as a wave broke near them. She braced herself against him. Unable to touch the bottom, she wrapped her legs around his hips.

"Trust me," she heard him say as she felt his breath on her lips. "I won't let us get in over our heads."

When his lips rocked softly against hers, she knew she was in over her head emotionally. She could rationalize the tiny bubbles of desire washing over her like air bubbles seeking the surface of the water. She could have dredged up a piece of medical information to explain the flash fire burning out of control inside of her; the sun's rays cause the brain to release a sexual hormone.

Yes, she could have explained the riot of emotions clamoring inside her, but she didn't.

She didn't think, period. She only felt.

Her lips parted beneath the increasing pressure of his mouth. His tongue seared across her, branding her with the taste of his soul. She met the velvet thrusts with light sips. Without speaking his tongue communicated his desire.

The promise of their being soul mates, the two people Hogan had loved most in the world, haunted both of them.

Rob wound the hair at her nape between his fingers as he reluctantly ended their kiss. He rocked his brow against hers, wondering if she could divine his thoughts as easily as she'd pretended to read the tea leaves.

"Do you think this is what Hogan really wanted when he made me his beneficiary?" he whispered huskily, speaking his thoughts aloud. "Matchmaking?"

"Hogan never tried to match me up with anyone else." She framed his face with her hands. "What's happening between us has nothing to do with Hogan's will."

"I'd have been attracted to you regardless of how or where we met."

Angelica grinned. "You sound as though you're trying to convince yourself of that fact."

"I am. Any man in the twentieth century would be bothered with the idea of someone else picking out his woman for him."

His woman? she silently repeated, relishing the words' possessiveness.

"Not to mention that he did it in such an eerie way," Rob added thoughtfully. "Hogan's sixth sense...his knowing when someone needed something before that person knew it. I don't believe in it. But do you realize we're probably doing exactly what he wanted?''

"Any choices being made are only the choices the two of us make. We're both educated, independent . . . too self-sufficient to believe Hogan is somewhere up there sprinkling love dust on us.''

Rob looked hard at her; she returned his stare. Simultaneously, they tossed back their heads and roared with laughter. Regardless of what they'd said, they both knew Hogan's gentle hand would have been nudging them together if he'd lived.

"We could call the ghostbusters," he teased, "but just between the two of us, I kind of like the idea of Hogan knowing we're friends.''

Angelica gave him a swift kiss and said, "I kind of like that idea, too.''

Six

Intent on Rob's transformation from stressed-out executive to lighthearted charmer, Angelica barely noticed when a cocky teenager sitting astride a surfboard let loose with an earsplitting wolf whistle. Laughing for no apparent reason, they waded toward the beach, hand-in-hand.

Blistering heat from the sugar sand under her bare feet should have served to distract Angelica. Tenderfooted, she usually imitated a cat on a hot tin roof getting back to her towel once she'd gone beyond the surf line. But this time her undivided attention was focused on Rob.

She dropped to her knees, not bothering to brush the sand off her feet before she stretched out on her towel. Her heart pumped double time, as though their leisurely stroll had been a marathon race. She'd always been attracted to Rob, but the effect he had on her when he wasn't worried sick was devastating!

The mind could only absorb a certain amount of external stimuli before it blew its conductors, she thought, admiring the masculine display of muscles beneath the droplets of water on Rob's shoulders and backside. Somewhere she'd read in a pop psychology article that a woman is attracted by a man's eyes, or his shoulders or his buns, not necessarily in that order. She grinned. Rob Emery had all three going for him.

"What's going on in that pretty head of yours?" Rob asked as he dropped beside her, lying on his side. He propped up his head on one arm. "You look like the kid who just ate the cherry at the bottom of her Shirley Temple."

She rolled to her side, facing him. "I'm enjoying the view."

"The...uh...ocean has the same effect on me, too." He grinned from ear to ear. His eyes moved appreciatively over her skimpy swimsuit.

"I wasn't looking at the ocean."

He leaned forward and dropped a kiss on the tip of her nose. "Neither was I."

Warmed by his sunny smile hovering a mere inch from her lips, she whispered, "I could get attached to that smile of yours."

"Feel free." That was precisely how he felt. Carefree.

She brushed her mouth against the curve of his lips. In a New York second, her shoulders were flat against her towel. Flecks of gold lit his eyes with an intense glow as his finger traced the bow of her bottom lip.

"We're on a public beach," he reminded himself aloud, wishing they were on a deserted island with no hope of rescue in the near future. His creative mind gave him the excuse he needed to touch her. He reached into her beach bag and withdrew the suntan lotion.

"Roll over. I'll do your back for you," he offered. While she rolled over, he twisted off the lid, then he dabbled a streak of white from one shoulder to the other. "I wouldn't want the sun to burn you."

Rays from the sun had warmed her; his fingers lazily coating her with the fragrance of coconut oil intensified the heat. Her eyes drifted closed. She savored each stroke as though it were a caress. When she felt lotion trickle down the backs of her thighs, behind her kneecaps, to her ankles, she opened her mouth to protest. She could do her legs. Her streak of independence wilted at the touch of his hand. One finger traced the vulnerable spot behind her knees, eliciting a silent moan of pleasure from her. She became malleable putty in his hands. He bent one leg, then the other to apply a liberal coat of protection to her feet and ankles.

"Shall I do your front?"

"Please."

Rolling to her back, she lay with her eyes wide open as she watched him squeeze the brown plastic bottle. A puddle began to form in the valley between her breasts where the bottle's spout had lingered the longest.

He wanted to dawdle, to dip his hands beneath the edge of her swimsuit, to feel the fullness of her breasts in his hands. One uninhibited finger of his dared to spread the puddle of lotion a fraction of an inch beneath her suit. Just to make certain there wasn't a burn line, he silently justified his boldness.

Sand sprayed over his feet when a youngster raced between the towels to reach the shoreline. "Sorry, mister."

"Me, too," Rob said with a sigh of regret.

Angelica heartily agreed. "Me, three. Ever hear of the pleasure-pain syndrome?"

"Uh-uh." He hadn't heard of it, but he sure as blazes was experiencing it. "Touching you without *really* touching you is a classic example, isn't it?"

"Mmm," she hummed. "I just made that up to describe what I'm feeling."

Her confession pleased him. He squeezed the bottle again, leaving a trail of lotion across her shins and up her thighs. "Want me to stop?"

"I'll give you an hour to quit." Propped up on her forearms, head thrown back, she let her eyes drift closed as his fingers painted seductive pictures on her legs. Cheeks flushed, she felt deliciously, wickedly feminine. "Maybe longer."

When his hands began to meticulously glide over her thighs, along her ankles, not sparing an inch of her legs from his ministration, her foot arched, digging her toes into the sand. Heat, stronger than the sun overhead, surged through her veins like liquid lava.

In his imagination, Rob mentally counted up the places he wanted to kiss. The tiny freckle on her shoulder blade. The crease behind her knees. The arch of her foot. Each toe. He realized he was letting his imagination drive him crazy.

For propriety's sake, he lobbed the bottle up beside her hand and stretched out on his stomach. His swim trunks seemed to have shrunk a size while he was touching her. That hadn't happened to him since he was a teenager. Come to think of it, during the past several months, maybe a year or so, he hadn't involuntarily reacted to being near a woman at all.

"Is that a self-satisfied grin I see?"

"Yep. Sure is."

"Why self-satisfied?"

"You wouldn't want to know."

"Psychiatrists want to know everything about—"

"I'm not your patient."

"Everything going on in everybody's mind," she finished, a little miffed that he wouldn't share his thoughts with her. Picking up the bottle, she painted a stripe down the hollow of his neck. "You can tell me anything. I'm trained not to be critical or judgmental."

Rob raised one eyelid. Hunched over his shoulders, she couldn't see the gleam of pure deviltry turning his eyes the color of a green traffic signal. She wants to crawl inside my skull and use it for a playground, he thought. I'll give her something shocking to play with.

"I'm a virgin," he crooned with the appropriate touch of sorrow laced in his voice.

Angelica wasn't fooled. She hadn't seen his eyes, but her hands could feel the laughter he suppressed in his chest. Did he think she'd forgotten about his offer to become friends and lovers? She'd given the idea a great deal of thought! Amused, she wondered exactly what had brought on such an outlandish statement.

She made her response as clinical as possible. "Oh. A virgin, hmm?"

"You aren't shocked?"

He tried to get a glimpse of her over his shoulder. Her fingers slid to his nape, which made turning his head impossible.

"No. Although I will admit that I hadn't pictured you as the shy type with women." Nor did she imagine that he lived in a monastery, where women weren't allowed. She closed her fingers around his neck in a strangle-

hold as she made a funny face. She had to give him
credit for ingenuity, she mused. He had a unique line for
coaxing a woman into his bed. If he wanted to play
mental games, she was more than willing. "Lack of sex
drive and stress—they're often close cousins."

Rob grinned. Immediately he felt her hands on his
shoulders giving him a light shake.

"What are you grinning about?"

"I was grinning because I think I'd like for you to be
the first woman I've slept with. I feel completely *un-
stressed*," he replied, steering her back on course. She'd
turned the tea leaf reading into tips to relieve stress. This
was his game; he'd make up the rules as they went
along.

You rascal, she mused, pummeling his back muscles
with harmless karate chops. "I've helped," she repeated, to let him know she'd listened. Encouraging him
to continue, she tacked on a melodious, "Weren't you
curious about sex as a teenager?"

"Yes," he answered honestly.

Whether he was telling the truth or not, she wasn't
going to let him know his claim of having been celibate
had a peculiar effect on her libido. She knew he was
joking, but the thought of him sleeping alone in his bed
pleased her. It also meant he wasn't emotionally involved with another woman.

She squirted a glob of lotion on the erogenous zone
behind his knees, and grinned at the knee-jerk reaction
as his heel raised toward her. Rob Emery had been under stress, but he was definitely a perfectly healthy
member of the male species.

She resisted the impulse to tweak the hairs on the
back of his leg. He had to know their attraction was
mutual. She wondered why he'd changed his tactics.

Maybe her refusal of his first offer had punctured his male ego. Or maybe he didn't make the same offer twice to the same woman. Could it be he was waiting for her to make the first move? Testing her last theory, she said deadpan, "I could help you solve that problem... completely."

Rob grinned and sat up. His conscience pricked him for tricking her into his bed, but he'd played the game to such perfection he deserved a reward, didn't he?

"I'll call the hospital and schedule some tests to be run," Angelica said, her eyes twinkling with mirth. "Maybe there's a physical problem."

He grabbed the sunscreen lotion and finished what she'd started. "You knew I was feeding you a line, didn't you?"

"Why, Rob..." Her eyes widened innocently. She lowered her voice to a thin whisper. "You mean you thought I swallowed the bait? Hook, line and you're a stinker!"

She ducked when his long arm reached for her. In an instant, she had her lime-green cover-up in her hand and was on her feet and running toward the water, laughing at his attempt to coax her into his bed. Little did he know that all he had to do was ask. She wanted him, without the time restrictions she'd placed on his first offer.

She flung her arms wide and pirouetted. Her cover-up flared in a wide circle as she chanted quietly, "I think I'm in love. I am in love." The ocean breeze caught her heart's refrain, tossed it to the four winds and carried it out to sea. She wanted the world to know how she felt. Before long, she promised, Rob would be let in on her little secret.

Rob stood at the edge of the towel, watching her sprint away from him and damning his own tactlessness. When he'd suggested they become lovers the first time, his mind had been cluttered with millions of strings tying him to New York. Now, with his second offer, she'd declined by calling him a stinker.

Only one other person had ever called him a stinker. Hogan had, the day they went sailing and Rob pretended he'd never set foot on a sailboat. Hogan had gotten even by falling overboard and taking Rob with him. Rob couldn't picture Hogan in a similar circumstance with a woman, but he wondered what Hogan would do.

Angelica was now spinning circles in the sand. She'd run from him, but she didn't appear angry. From where he stood, she looked exhilarated. And damned precious, he silently added.

A slow grin spread across his face as he recalled what Hogan had said the couple of times he'd been caught in an outrageous story. It might work, Rob mused, starting after Angelica. Considering the fact that he'd already given her the one and only pink satin flamingo in Oviedo to make amends for his last series of mistakes, it had to work.

Angelica played tag with the waves, racing toward them as they receded, running backward as they surged forward. Once or twice she glanced over her shoulder to see what Rob was up to.

Uh-oh, she thought, when she caught sight of him jogging toward her with a king-size gator grin plastered on his face. He's up to something. Water swirled around her ankles and the wave sucked grains of sand from beneath her feet. Neither had the same dizzy effect his smile had on her.

"What I told you is true," Rob said without preliminary. "Except for a lie or two thrown in on the spur of the moment."

When he winked, Angelica could have sworn it was Hogan winking at her.

Mesmerized, she advanced toward him. "'Honesty begets honesty,'" she said, quoting Rob's uncle. "I'm halfway in love with you, Rob Emery. If it scares you, tell me now."

His arms opened wide. She slipped between them. His fingers twined together low on her spine; her hands circled his waist, completing a circle of love. He kissed the top of her head.

"You want commitment. I can't promise you forever," he murmured in complete truthfulness.

"Promise me today and tonight." She lifted her chin until their eyes met. "We'll let the tomorrows take care of themselves."

Seven

He stared at her, wanting to believe his good fortune, but deathly afraid he'd misunderstood her. "I have to go back to New York. My life's work is there."

"I know. And I also know the old idiom about absence making the heart grow fonder is statistically inaccurate."

His fingers brushed a strand of windblown hair back from her face. Glib reassurances withered on his tongue as he gazed into her eyes. When the joke was on himself, he could stretch the truth. But Angelica was special to him. He couldn't reveal how special without building false hopes.

"You aren't a woman a man could easily forget, Angelica. My offer for you to join me in New York still holds good." He laced his fingers through hers and began slowly walking along the shore. "You don't belong on a gator farm."

She dismissed his offer and his opinion with a shake of her head. Gallantry was a puny substitute for commitment. "Sometimes late at night I stare at the ceiling and wonder why I became part of Hogan's scheme to preserve one little corner of the world."

"And?"

She grinned. "Remember the fairy tale, *Snow White and the Seven Dwarfs*?"

"Sleepy, Dopey and their pint-size associates? Yeah, I remember."

"I picture myself in the leading role, languishing, half-asleep in Hogan's tropical splendor, waiting to be awakened." She chuckled and lightly squeezed his fingertips. "I don't know if your kiss awakened me, but you certainly arouse me."

"I'm no prince," he flatly denied.

"That depends on your definition of a prince. In Hogan's little kingdom you are the heir apparent. Doesn't that make you a prince?"

"What it makes me is an absentee landlord."

Angelica tapped him in the ribs with her elbow. "Where's your romanticism?"

"Buried under tons of steel, concrete and television cables. Can you imagine what would happen if I advertised Hogan's property as a kingdom and tried to pass myself off as a prince? I'd be zapped with a lawsuit for false advertising quicker than you could say bibbety-bobbety-boo." As he uttered the magical words, he stopped and pointed to a crowd of sunbathers forming a near perfect line a hundred yards ahead. "What's going on over there?"

"It's probably some sort of beach contest. The last time I was here the muscle-bound beach boys were having a weight lifting contest, while their female counterparts were strutting their stuff in the tiniest bikinis I've ever seen." She tugged on his hand. "Let's go see."

As they drew closer they could hear the appreciative oohs and aahs of the milling crowd. Angelica noticed several little tykes, no older than three or four, toting buckets of wet sand to the inner edge of the line.

"Must be a sand castle contest," she guessed, edging between the onlookers.

"Sand painting, too," said an elderly lady clad in a wide-brimmed straw hat and protective clothing from her neck to her knees. She pointed farther up the line. "That one over there is my favorite."

Angelica's eyes followed the direction of the woman's manicured finger to where a sand artist picked up a plastic bottle and began carefully pouring glittering red and gold sand above a monstrous-sized dragon's nostrils. With a swirl of the artist's fingers, the dragon appeared to be breathing fire.

"That's my grandson," the woman added with pride in her voice. "He's going to be a fine artist some day."

Rob nodded, amazed by what the artists had created on a canvas of sand: everything from lifelike ocean creatures to mythological dragons. Presiding nearby were castles complete with moats, turrets and flags.

"Want to give it a try?" Angelica asked, looking up at Rob's face, where wistfulness was clearly visible.

Tempted, he hesitated, then asked, "What's the entry fee?"

"There's no charge for a stretch of empty beach."

"And the prize?"

Inwardly, Angelica groaned. "A million dollars' worth of self-satisfaction, with an additional bonus of giving other people pleasure."

"A handcrafted, Cocoa Beach tie-dyed T-shirt," the older woman corrected, chuckling at the younger woman's response. "Something to wipe the sweat off your brow if you're lucky enough to win."

"Best of luck to your grandson," Rob said politely, towing Angelica farther up the line.

"You aren't going to give it a try?"

"In front of all these people? No thanks. I wouldn't have a chance of winning."

Angelica rolled her eyes toward the sky. "You're hopeless."

"No, but I am competitive. I like to win. Show me somebody who doesn't enjoy the thrill of winning and I'll show you a loser."

She groaned aloud. "Everything isn't a win-or-lose proposition."

"Before you get up on your psychological soapbox, let's simply agree to disagree. It's too hot to fight. Okay?"

"Okay. I'll agree to disagree on one condition," she stipulated. "I have the compelling urge to build a sand castle. Not here, where everybody's watching, but farther down the beach at the waterline."

Rob looped his arm across her shoulders and gave her a quick hug. "To prove your point?"

"Just for fun. I promise not to breathe another word about your being overly competitive. Please?"

"A small sand castle," he acquiesced with a wide grin.

With the diligence of master architects, they scavenged an assortment of paper cups from a trash barrel while heatedly discussing the best location for their castle, what to use for a drawbridge and how high the castle's wall should be. They decided on a spot fifteen

SUNSHINE

yards from the water's edge, Popsicle sticks for the drawbridge, and they mutually agreed to wait until the castle was built to determine how high to make the wall.

Once the major decisions were made, Angelica was surprised by how well they worked together. For each trip she made to get wet sand for the foundation, Rob lugged his share of sand-filled cups. When she offered suggestions, based on her previous experience building castles, he listened attentively, followed her advice and then added creative touches.

They completely lost track of time. The sun reached its apex and had tracked across the sky until it was partially hidden behind the high-rise condos bordering the beach. Mothers and fathers had rounded up their broods, packed up their cars and were returning to their homes. Only a few sunbaked stragglers roamed the beach searching for shells.

Rob sat back on his haunches to survey their work. What had started out as the small castle he'd stipulated had grown to be three feet tall and equally as wide. Small shells decorated the turrets; larger shells provided footpaths for the nonexistent nobility.

Angelica wiped the bead of sweat from her upper lip as she began burrowing a hole at the base.

"What are you doing?"

"Digging a secret escape tunnel. All castles have them." She peeked over the rows of flags, made of paper wrapped around toothpicks, and said, "Every castle has to have a tunnel. You start from that side. Be careful or it'll cave in."

"Why don't we pretend there is a tunnel, then we won't have to worry about it caving in," he suggested, not wanting to take a chance on their workmanship being destroyed.

"Uh-uh. It won't collapse if you dip your fingers in water and pat the sides as you go along."

On hands and knees he crawled to her side. "Watch out. It's going to . . ." He jackknifed to his feet and ran to the water, cup in hand.

"Oops."

With one hand deep in sand and the other patting the rapidly deteriorating wall, she decided to take his suggestion. Ever so slowly she started to back her hand from the hole she'd dug.

"Here." Rob dropped flat on his belly and trickled water down her wrist. "Easy. Easy does it. Slosh it around a little."

Angelica smirked, wondering how he'd react if she yanked her hand out. For a man who wasn't interested in building a castle unless there was adequate compensation, he acted as though he was saving the Empire State Building from destruction!

With infinite care she extracted her fingers from the tunnel. His sigh of relief was music to her ears. A man who fights to preserve a sand castle is worthy of hero worship, she mused.

Her wet, sand-encrusted hand slipped around his waist as her other arm closed around his neck for a prolonged bear hug. She felt the side of his face contort into a wince. Only then did she realize the price he'd paid for their castle. In their enthusiasm, they'd both forgotten to reapply coats of sunscreen.

She peered over his shoulder as she removed her hands. White imprints where she'd touched him were clearly visible. Leaning backward, she scanned his face. He wrinkled his nose, then grinned.

"What's a little sunburn?" he said, amiably dismissing the feeling that his skin had caught fire. He rose, bringing her with him. He resisted the temptation to pull her snugly against him. His chest, stomach and legs were as tender as his back. "It only hurts when I laugh."

"You should have said something." Terrible guilt pangs ricocheted through her. She'd been sneaking peeks at him the entire afternoon. Why hadn't she realized his skin was turning pink? Angelica knew the answer to that question. She'd been too busy daydreaming about sharing a castle with him to keep track of realities.

"I didn't notice. I was having too much fun." He stepped backward. The flesh behind his kneecaps stung. His grin slipped into being a wry grimace. "Correction. It only hurts when I laugh, stand, walk and breathe. Other than those minor inconveniences, I feel absolutely great."

"Let's get you home. A cool bath in tea should give you immediate relief." Despite his sunburn, he did look happier, healthier than he had upon his arrival. "I'm afraid you're going to peel from head to toe."

Rob would have shrugged off her comment, but the skin across his shoulders revolted at the idea. He helped her gather the towels, neatly folding them and shoving them into her beach bag. The barely used bottle of suntan oil seemed to mock him as he tucked it in the beach bag's front pocket.

One look at his front, then another over his shoulder at his backside quelled the fantasies he'd woven while they were building the sand castle. Florida's sun had set him aflame instead of Angelica's soft hands. His big plans to woo and win her would go right down the drain with his bathwater.

"Are you in pain?" Angelica asked as she watched the muscle along his jaw harden.

"No." *Yes! Mental anguish!* As he stepped on the boardwalk that crossed over the sand dunes, he leaned against the rail and raised his right leg to inspect the sensitized sole of his foot. Air whistled through his teeth. "They're sunburned, too!"

"Do you want to stop at the drugstore on the way home to pick up something for it?"

Medicine would only give him temporary relief, he thought, shaking his head. What he needed the most he couldn't possibly get from a spray can of medication. "No thanks."

Before he took another step, he turned toward the beach. The tide had turned. Waves rushed against the shore, threatening to undermine the foundation of the castle. His mind's eye took a snapshot.

"Sand castles aren't meant to last forever," he reminded himself a bit sadly.

Angelica heard the pensive note in his voice. "We can build another. Next time we'll bring sand buckets and shovels...." Her plans for the future died in the back of her throat where a knot formed. She couldn't count on there being a next time. Her eyes lingered on the flags that jauntily waved their goodbyes as the surf crashed over them. She swallowed hard. "It was beautiful while it lasted."

"A real prizewinner," Rob agreed, glancing up at the darkening horizon to clear the moisture from his eyes. Dammit! He was too old to get teary-eyed over a sand castle's being demolished by waves. In genuine fear of making a fool of himself, he took Angelica by the elbow and turned her away from the beach. Without premeditation, he rashly promised, "Next year we'll enter the contest. I've always wanted to win a Cocoa Beach tie-dyed T-shirt.''

A couple of hours later, semirecuperated after soaking in a tub filled with Angelica's special mixture of tea water and herbs, Rob wrapped a towel below his waist and gingerly hobbled into his bedroom.

"Better?" Angelica asked, glancing over her shoulder as she turned down the sheets of his bed. She held up the bottle of sun-relief lotion. "Do you want me to do your back?"

While he was bathing, she'd gone back to her house, taken a quick shower, changed into a white jumpsuit and returned with a bottle of ointment guaranteed to take the sting out of a sunburn.

"No, thanks." His jade eyes darkened as the black centers widened, skimming over her feminine curves. "Having you tuck me into bed isn't how I'd hoped to end the evening."

Flustered by the idea that he must have read her mind, she dropped her eyes from the band of terry cloth at his waist to his dark pink ankles and said, "Oh?"

"Yeah. Oh." Ouch was what he would be bellowing if he wrapped his arm around her and tumbled them both into bed. He touched his forearm, hoping for instant recuperative powers. White fingerprints induced a shiver that prohibited him from throwing caution to the winds. "I don't suppose this will miraculously go away between here and the bed, will it?"

Angelica shook her head. She stepped backward until the dresser pressed against her rear. She'd rummaged through his drawers and had been unable to find any pajamas. He slept nude. The thought of him dropping his towel before he slid between the sheets had her inching toward the door.

Modesty or temptation? she wondered, twining a lock of hair between her fingers. Her thumb worried across the silky texture to soothe her frazzled nerves. Unaware of it, she painted the tips across her cheek. She honestly didn't know which motivated her urge to make a hasty retreat, but she wasn't going to stick around long enough to find out.

"No, I don't think so. A good night's sleep should help, though." Her hand touched the doorknob; she twisted it and opened the door. "G'night, Rob. Sweet dreams."

For a man whose soles of his feet were tender to the touch, he crossed the room with amazing agility. He grinned at the astonishment on her face, then audaciously puckered his lips, demanding a good-night kiss. Physically, he couldn't do more, but he sure as hell wasn't going to have less.

Careful to keep from touching him, she rose on tiptoes until her lips met his. All the yearning she'd felt as she'd showered and dressed poured into her chaste kiss.

Her heels touched the floor as he whispered, "I'll be dreaming of you, sweet lady."

Unable to resist the dewiness of her lips, he slanted his mouth over hers for a second kiss. Remnants of her chaste kiss vaporized as his tongue hotly pierced her parted lips. His fingers splayed into her hair, turning her head as he tantalized her into returning his kiss.

She followed the velvet tip of his tongue as it receded. Her tongue swirled in tiny, erotic circles against his. The sweet taste of his leashed desire flooded her senses. She heard his low groan, felt his hand tighten in her hair. Her knees threatened to buckle. She couldn't touch him without hurting him. Her hands moved to the only place his skin had been untouched by the sun, to the towel on his hips.

"Angelica . . ." He whispered her name like a prayer across her lips. "I want you."

Sanity, a commodity in increasingly short supply, made Angelica's heels drop back to the floor. His sigh of frustration matched the one she swallowed. Weak-willed from desire, she couldn't move farther away from him.

Rob dropped his hands to his sides and had the strength to take a step back toward the bed. "Sweet dreams, Angelica. I'll be dreaming of you, sweet lady."

She slipped through the bedroom door, closing it softly behind her. Lock it, she silently ordered Rob. She wasn't prone toward sleepwalking, but she wasn't certain he'd be safe from her if his door remained unlocked.

Figaro rubbed against her legs, drawing her attention downward.

"Feeling left out in the cold?" she asked softly. She scooped the cat up in her arms. Instantly, Figaro began purring loudly. "Don't worry. It's just you and me, kitty-o."

Purely for her own precautionary reasons, she locked his front door as she left.

Once they were inside her house, Figaro jumped from her arms. Angelica flicked the light switch upward. Regally, the cat hoisted her tail to full mast and padded to the empty food bowl in the kitchen.

"Don't you give me that pitiful I'm-starving-to-death look." She shook her finger, scolding. "For a persnickety cat who turns her nose up at dried cat food, you must have been munching away the whole day while Rob and I were at the beach. What's with you?"

Figaro crouched down, hissing at the pink satin flamingo perched in the dinette window.

"Jealous? That's ridiculous. You never sit in that window."

Stalking her prey, Figaro edged toward the interloper.

"Oh no, you don't." Quicker than the cat, Angelica grabbed Rob's present. She hugged it to her chest protectively. "You keep your claws off this."

With wide-eyed innocence, Figaro sniffed, then strolled back to her food bowl.

"I know you're pretending not to notice what I do with it." She placed the flamingo on top of the refrigerator for safekeeping. "Don't you know possessiveness is an outward sign of insecurity? Don't expect me to overindulge you with food just because Rob didn't bring you a present. You have plenty of toys that Hogan gave you."

Figaro's submissive meow didn't deceive Angelica.

"Don't you dare climb up on the refrigerator or you'll be in big trouble." She crossed to the cupboard below the sink. "A few crunchies. That's it until morning."

She poured the food into Figaro's bowl. "I love you, too," she whispered reassuringly, stroking the cat with genuine fondness. "Yeah, I love him, Figaro. But you know what Hogan said about sunshine and love— there's plenty for everybody."

She chuckled. Rob had gotten too much of one and she'd gotten too little of the other. Hogan's homespun philosophy obviously didn't apply in all cases.

Rob stared up at the ceiling. For what seemed like hours he'd willed his mind to stop flying nonstop between New York and Orlando, Orlando and New York. His intense desire to be with Angelica complicated his scheme to free the alligators as quickly as possible and return to New York.

Angelica, he thought. Where had she been back in college when he was eager to find "the perfect woman"? Back then, he'd searched for a woman to share his dreams. Aside from a few flings at purposely trying to fall in love, his heart had remained intact. Why had fate put her in his path at this inopportune moment?

"Fate, thy name is Hogan?" he mused aloud, remembering the mysterious letter that had accompanied his uncle's last will and testament. "His sixth sense didn't have anything to do with my arriving at a crossroad in my life. Hogan had a blueprint in his back pocket!"

Until he received Hogan's letter, there'd been only one direction in his life—straight to the top of Lockey, Stearnes and Cordell advertising agency. If his growth was stunted, it wasn't his professional growth. The psychological exam he'd take once he returned to New York was a hurdle, not a barricade. He could pass it with flying colors.

An image of brightly colored strips of paper flying atop a sand castle and a beautiful woman twirling on one foot threatened to distract Rob from his train of thought.

"Where was I?" He hated being absentminded more than he disliked the flights of fantasy he had while in the middle of solving a problem. "Oh, yeah. Hogan's letter. Crossroads."

Thanks to his dearly departed uncle and his gator farm, he'd met and fallen hard for Angelica. Had Hogan intentionally shot Cupid's arrow in his direction by saying there was something of more value than money and success in the pot of gold at the end of the rainbow? Did he mean Angelica? Was Rob's falling for her part of Hogan's overall plan?

Rob felt certain that listening to his heart wouldn't lead him back to New York. His office was sixteen floors above ground level, but during rush hour traffic there were times when he could barely hear himself think, much less listen to his heart.

"Hogan, you old scoundrel, you sent me a subliminal sales pitch! Before I arrived in Florida, you had me wondering if I'd missed something in life. Lo and behold, you bequeath me your estate, I fly down here . . . and who appears out of the darkness? Angelica! Your idea of precisely what's missing in my life."

Satisfied that he'd solved the mystery shrouding Hogan's letter, he grinned. Sixth sense—humbug. Damned good advertising practices was more like it. Discover a man's secret fantasy, then wrap your product in his illusions—the essence of the advertising business.

Hogan must have wanted to find a suitable partner for Angelica and I was the lucky consumer!

Although the night air wafting through the windows was hot and sultry, Rob shivered. Cautious of his tender skin, he reached down and pulled the sheet across himself. Thirty seconds later he kicked it off as beads of perspiration formed on his upper lip.

He had found the only logical reason behind Hogan's letter, hadn't he?

Again, the picture of a woman dancing for joy near a sand castle penetrated through his logic. Angelica's melodious laughter echoed in his ears.

He flopped from one side of the bed to the other, but the image and the sound refused to fade. He willed his subconscious to make them a living part of his dreams. His mind continued to work overtime.

Giving up on falling asleep, he slowly moved to the edge of the bed. What he needed, other than Angelica Franklin beside him in bed, was a drink of water.

Deciding the calluses on his heels were less tender than the balls of his feet, he crossed awkwardly to the closet to get his robe. Off balance, he jarred his shoulder against the doorjamb as he swung the door open. Over the sound of his muffled curses, he heard a peculiar squeaking noise, like rusty hinges on a gate.

"Figaro?" he called, choosing to believe the cat had managed to get inside the closet rather than let his imagination run wild to the other creatures inhabiting the tropical forest surrounding the house.

He pulled on the cord attached to the naked light bulb in the closet. His eyes adjusted to the light, then moved from left to right, from the empty shelves overhead to the suitcase on the floor. He pushed his clothes to one side, then stared at the waist-high door at the back of the closet. Angelica had mentioned the necessity for every sand castle to have a secret passage, but surely the local philanthropist didn't need an escape route.

Privacy, Rob speculated. When Hogan had visited Rob and his parents, there had been times when he'd go up into the attic to be alone with his dreams. The only time Hogan had given Rob a disapproving look had been when Rob had dared to invade his privacy by sneaking up the attic ladder in search of his uncle.

"A man has to have a special place to create his dreams," he'd said gruffly.

When Hogan built this house, had he provided himself with a special dream room?

Rob examined the old-fashioned latch. Somehow, his shoulder ramming against the doorframe must have knocked it from its place. He widened the opening with a light kick.

Rob had outgrown his fear of darkness decades ago, but he staunchly rejected the idea of blundering into a pitch-black abyss without a flashlight. He completely forgot about his tender feet as he strode into the kitchen. He'd seen a flashlight in one of the drawers. Systematically, he looked in each of the cabinet drawers until he found it.

With the flick of a switch, he tested the batteries. They worked. A strong beam of light preceded him back into the closet.

"Let's see what we've got here," he mumbled, dropping down on all fours.

He winced as his kneecaps touched the hardwood floor. So what've we got here, Hogan, he asked silently, bouncing the beam around a room no larger than ten-by-ten.

Curiosity sparked his sense of adventure. He crawled through the aperture. He expected the musky odor of mildew, cobwebs, dust and Lord only knew what else. His flashlight revealed a tidy room.

Rob got to his feet, lifting the light toward the ceiling. A patch of starlit sky, no bigger than a television screen, was what he saw.

"There has to be a light switch in here somewhere." He circled the beam around the walls until he found what he searched for. He pulled on a metal chain dangling beneath a light fixture. "Well, I'll be damned," he whispered, feeling as though he'd stumbled into a bank vault.

Covering the counter running the width of the room were Hogan's watercolor paintings in various stages of completion. His eyes widened fractionally as they moved to an easel propped in the far corner. Stiff-legged, he moved until he stood directly in front of a painting of a man and boy. He leaned closer, unable to believe his eyes. His finger skimmed over the two figures.

There was no mistaking the Cheshire-cat grin on the old man's wrinkled face, nor could Rob mistake the identity of the green-eyed child sheltered under Hogan's arm. At first glance, both figures appeared to be walking on clouds. Muted pastels swirled behind them in two-thirds of the composition. On closer inspection, Rob realized Hogan hadn't finished the painting.

Given a million years to explain why he reached for the cup filled with paintbrushes, Rob would have been unable to make a reasonable explanation. He hadn't touched a palette of paints since he'd emptied the box Hogan gave him. Perhaps seeing the work of other artists at the beach provided the source of his inspiration. Possibly the creative urge stemmed from the mental picture in his mind that spurned his attempts to be eradicated by logic. Or it might have been the creative half of his brain kicking into high gear, demanding satisfaction long denied.

Before Rob was consciously aware of what he was doing, he'd filled several small jars with water from the faucet in the bathroom, moved the easel beside the workbench stool and begun mixing watercolors on a paper plate. Finishing Hogan's painting would be extremely difficult, but he was determined to recall every technique his uncle had taught him.

He practiced his brush stroke time and time again on a pad of paper. A tiny bit of color washed with water, he mentally recited. Light strokes. Don't scrub the bristles of the brush. Let the tip of the brush do the work for you.

He covered one page with strokes. Dissatisfied, he turned to the next sheet. What would have been sheer frustration to a less determined man became a challenge to Rob. He simply had to finish what Hogan had started.

Eight

Angelica waited until a respectable hour of the morning to go over to Rob's house with a plate of freshly baked biscuits and a jar of homemade blueberry jam. She grinned as one of Rob's "lawnmowers" bellowed a wake-up call. Lightly she tapped on the front door.

"Rob? It's me." She opened the screen and tried the knob, then remembered she'd locked it before leaving last night. She knocked harder, and raised her voice a decibel. "Unlock the door, would you?"

She turned her ear toward the door to listen for movement inside the house. Out of the corner of her eye she noticed Rob's rental car still parked in the drive. He had to be there. Why wasn't he answering the door? She'd heard of visitors unaccustomed to the Florida sun who'd had sunstrokes, but she felt fairly certain she'd have noticed symptoms of heat prostration.

"He must be sound asleep," she deduced, resigning herself to returning to her house and sharing her breakfast with Figaro.

She glanced up at the sun. It was probably between nine and ten. He'd had at least twelve hours' sleep. To make certain he was sleeping and not ill, she circled the corner of the house and strode toward the bedroom window.

Her concern warred with the knowledge that Rob slept nude. Was she a Peeping Tomasina or a Florence Nightingale? she silently asked herself. Uncertain whether her motivation was purely selfless, she set the food on the ground, broke off a dead twig from a nearby bush and tapped on a pane of glass with it. She backed up and waited for him to come to the window.

Her bright, good-morning smile faded with each second she waited. Her brow furrowed into worry lines. She could be mistaken about his not being ill. To hell with puritanical modesty, she decided, moving to the window. Her peace of mind was at stake.

"Empty?" she murmured, staring at the bed, but not quite accepting the fact that Rob wasn't there. "So where is he?"

Pivoting on the ball of her foot, she cast her eyes around the immediate area. He had to be somewhere on the property. The only likely place she could think of was the gator ponds. He knew they had to be fed today. That mile-wide streak of I-can-do-it-by-myself in his psyche must have prompted him to decide to feed them.

She picked up the biscuits and jam, then walked around to the front porch. He had a head start on her. She put the food on the porch. She could jog faster empty-handed. After she helped him with the feeding, they could come back to his place for a leisurely breakfast.

"That is, if he still has an appetite."

Her nose wrinkled at the thought of Rob entering the shed where the alligator food was stored in commercial freezers. Only a dedicated fisherman or a person with a severe head cold could handle the frozen blocks of fish, nutria and vitamin supplements without being tempted to hold his nose.

She started off on the path leading to the ponds, confident that Rob would enthusiastically welcome a pair of helping hands.

Startled awake by a tapping noise, Rob lifted his head from his arms. Momentarily disoriented, he thought he'd fallen asleep at his desk in his office until his eyes focused on the wadded sheets of paper strewn across the worktable. Stiff and sore, he lightly placed his hands on the small of his back and gave a jaw-popping yawn.

A slow smile of satisfaction curved his mouth as he turned toward the painting he'd completed. Sunlight from the skylight overhead lit the vibrant colors he'd added. The painting was as close to perfection as Rob could make it. Hogan wore his scruffy tennis shoes, with one shoelace untied, and the child was barefooted, a condition strictly forbidden around the Emery household. Only when he was with Hogan had Rob been able to shed his shoes.

Shutting his eyes, Rob could almost feel the blades of grass he'd painted growing beneath his feet. He'd forgotten those carefree summer days he spent roaming the countryside with his uncle. While he finished the painting during the wee hours of the morning, he'd dredged them up from his memory.

He realized he hadn't always agreed with his mother's negative opinion of her brother. Hogan's unexpected visits were bright spots in his regimented life. Hogan had told him that petty rules, like those requiring that one eat watermelon with a fork and chew bubble gum quietly, were meant to be broken. Hogan could spit watermelon seeds forty feet; he could blow a bubble bigger than his entire face.

Rob had admired Hogan. It felt good to know now for certain that Hogan was worthy of his childhood admiration. After listening to Angelica and the townspeople of Oviedo, Rob realized that if his mother looked down her nose and asked, "Do you want to turn out like your uncle?" he'd shout, "Yes!"

Giving credit where credit was due, he picked up an India ink pen off the worktable. Boldly, he lettered Hogan's initials at the bottom of the painting. In less conspicuous lettering tucked amid the blades of grass, he signed Hogan's nickname for him—Scutes.

Saturated with feelings of accomplishment and self-satisfaction, he returned to the bedroom, eager to tell Angelica of the treasure he'd discovered behind the closet wall. He considered using the telephone to invite her over, but decided against it. He wanted to see her face light up with pleasure.

Anxious to see her, he hurried into the bathroom to shave. He'd completely forgotten about his sunburn until he glanced in the mirror. The skin across the bridge of his nose and cheekbones had a pinkish tinge, but the soreness was gone. Whatever magical herbs Angelica had added to the tea and put in his bathwater, they had worked wonders. His arms and legs were already turning an olive brown.

"How 'bout that tan, Earl? Mike Lombardo's Hawaiian tan will be pale in comparison."

Rob inwardly cringed at the competitive thought. He absolutely refused to let Lockey, Stearnes and Cordell infringe on his high spirits. He still had the better part of his vacation in front of him. He planned to enjoy it to the hilt!

Angelica searched for signs of Rob having followed the path as she unhooked the string of wire from the gatepost. Maybe he's in the shed passed out from asphyxiation, she mused with wicked delight. She'd be more than happy to revive him with the kiss of life.

She followed the trail beyond the gator ponds toward the shed. Wire grass and marsh fleabane growing unchecked made the going tougher. During the months of May and June, while the gators were courting and nesting, the natural vegetation was allowed to invade the area to provide cover, nesting material and shade. Throughout the remainder of the year the pen had to be mowed.

From the frequency and volume of the mating calls, she figured it would be only two or three weeks before she'd be harvesting alligator eggs. Ideally, the eggs needed to be collected as soon after the laying as possible.

Near the man-made hill where the shed was located, she called, "Rob? Are you in there?"

Arnie's full-blown bellow was the only response she heard.

She climbed the mound and unlatched the door. She always hosed down the concrete floor in the shed after each feeding, but fish odor still hung heavily on the air. Reflexively, she waved her hand under her nose.

Rob was nowhere to be seen.

He wasn't at the house, she thought. He isn't at the feed shed. So where is he?

"Okay! Okay!" she shouted when Arnie broke loose with another earsplitting bellow. Being the biggest of the gators, he was also the hungriest—the amount of food an alligator consumed being directly proportional to its body weight. Arnie's appetite exceeded even his measurements. A glutton, he'd overeat and then suffer from gout. "Stop your complaining. I'll feed you, but you aren't getting out with the females."

For the next half hour, she pondered over where Rob could possibly have gone, while she filled five-gallon buckets with blocks of ground fish, nutria and vitamins. She was just about to heave the buckets onto a wagon when the door creaked on its hinges.

"Whew-eee!" Rob said, pinching his nostrils together as he stepped inside the shed. "This place stinks like a cat food factory. How do you keep Figaro away from here?"

"I don't." She nodded toward the noisy gator ponds. "They do. Figaro is no fool."

He lowered his hand to the bucket handle, pushing her hand aside. "I'll load the wagon. I told you I wanted to learn everything about the alligator farm operation. Why didn't you wait for me?"

"I did. I banged on your door and tapped on the bedroom window." Angelica brushed a damp lock of hair off her forehead with the back of her arm. She crossed to the utility sink to wash her hands. Teasing him, she asked, "Where were you? Hiding in the closet to keep out of the sun?"

Rob chuckled softly. "Yep. I was in the closet, more or less, but it wasn't to avoid the sun. Whatever kind of magical potion you slipped into my bathwater last night worked miracles."

His laughter sounded good to her ears. It wasn't rusty from disuse as it had been the first time she heard it. Her heart skipped a beat in anticipation as he held out his bare arms for her inspection. Angelica resisted the impulse to leave her mark on him by pressing her damp fingertips against his skin.

"Aloe," she whispered, naming the succulent plant she'd squeezed the juices from to relieve the sting of his sunburn.

"Since you've shared the name of the secret ingredient with me, I feel honor bound to share one with you." Rob dropped his hands to the wagon handle. He rolled it out of the shed. "Did you know there's a secret room in Hogan's house?"

"No. Where?" She moved beside him on the path to keep the gator food downwind from her. "What did you find?"

"One question at a time. It's located behind the closet in the bedroom. And—" he paused dramatically "—it's filled with treasure."

Angelica knew he had to be pulling her leg, but she played along with his story. "Oh, yeah? Gold and silver? Diamonds and emeralds?"

"Rare paintings. Extremely valuable."

"As in Picasso, Rembrandt and Van Gogh?" she teased, barely able to keep a straight face.

"Nope. Hogan painted them."

"I'd like to see them." Grinning up at him, she fairly burst with pride at his change of attitude. There was definitely hope for a man who wanted to free the gators and build sand castles and who considered Hogan's paintings valuable. She had to restrain herself from giving him a bear hug.

Aware of the spontaneous combustion that occurred inside of her from the most casual of touches, her superego filtered the messages her id sent. Hands off him. Talk about the weather, alligators, the cost of peanut butter in Yugoslavia, but don't touch him.

Eager to get finished with their work, she lengthened her stride. "Arnie has seniority around here. He gets fed first."

"How much?"

"Approximately six percent of his body weight."

Rob frowned. "Don't tell me we have to get Arnie on a set of bathroom scales before we feed him."

"According to his length, I'd say he weighs about four hundred pounds." She did Rob's mental calculations for him. "Twenty-four pounds of food. Each filled bucket weighs twenty-five pounds. The feeding station is at the back of his pen."

"That seems like a starvation diet for a critter his size."

"Feed him too much and he'll get gout. Then he has to fast for ten days to cure it. Believe me, an alligator on a restricted diet is one disagreeable beast."

Rob hoisted one bucket off the wagon and strode to the back of the pen. "Chow time, Arnie."

Arnie continued basking in the sun, oblivious to the man speaking to him.

"Did I do something wrong?"

"Uh-uh. He's wary of you."

"The feeling is mutual," Rob grunted, estimating the weight of food left in the bottom of the bucket to be about a pound. "Where to next?"

In the following hour, Rob did the heavy labor while Angelica gave him a crash course of feeding, fertility rates and egg collection to keep her mind off the way his back muscles strained against the fabric of his shirt as he worked. She had to mentally slap her hand to stop it from wiping the perspiration from his brow with the cloth in her back pocket. Rob and she had cleaned up and were heading back toward the house when he began quizzing her in earnest, taxing her powers of concentration.

"How many eggs in each nest?"

"Thirty-six to forty-two. They should be collected the first day, if possible. Each egg has to be marked for upright orientation, otherwise they won't hatch."

"What happens if a breeder waits until all the eggs are laid before he harvests them?"

"The hatcheries can determine an alligator's sex, male or female, by the temperature maintained between the seventh and twenty-first days of the incubation period. Since males grow larger, faster, the breeders make more money off males."

"How long before the first eggs are laid here?"

Angelica shrugged. "My guess is it'll be about two or three weeks. Hogan used to gather the eggs, but I can manage."

The thought of her robbing the nests with irate female alligators nearby sent chills up his spine. "Isn't that dangerous?"

"Not if you know what you're doing."

"Do you think there's much chance of our setting them free before they lay their eggs?"

"None." The worried frown marring his brow told her that he was concerned for her safety. She'd held herself in check long enough, she decided, placing a reassuring hand on his arm as they climbed the front steps of his house. His fingers folded over her hand. "I'll be fine. I promise I won't take any chances."

"I'm convinced you know the ins and outs of gator farming, but I'd feel better if I were here."

She would, too, but for a purely selfish reason that had nothing to do with hunting alligator eggs.

"Don't worry, okay?"

For the sake of being amiable, he nodded his head in agreement. He would worry, but not in her presence. Before he left for New York, he'd make some sort of arrangements for the care of the alligators.

Angelica glanced toward the corner of the porch where she'd put the biscuits and jam. Only the jar remained untouched. The plate was empty, licked clean of crumbs. Without a second thought, she knew who the guilty culprit was.

"Figaro! Where are you?" She stomped loudly to the end of the porch in case the cat was hiding under there. She picked up the plate. Over her shoulder, she said to Rob, "She ate your breakfast."

As Rob opened the screen door, the cat bolted between his legs before he could scissor them together. Guilty as sin, she hotfooted it into the palmettos to escape being scolded.

"Figaro! How in the world did you get *inside* the house?" Angelica asked.

She would have darted down the steps after the cat, but Rob wrapped an arm around her waist. "I don't eat breakfast, remember?"

You should, she meant to say, but Rob turned her around and brushed a kiss on her mouth. A warm rush of heat, like sunshine on a gator's scutes, made her swallow her opinion. She emptied her hands by leaning backward to put the plate and jar on the wicker rocking chair.

Her fingers walked up the front of his shirt until they met at the back of his collar. "What was that for?" she asked huskily.

"Me." His hands slipped low on her back. "I've been wanting to kiss you for the past two hours. Saving Figaro's hide was just the excuse I needed."

She reached up on tiptoe to nibble on his bottom lip. "You don't need an excuse. Feel free to kiss me any time the urge strikes you."

"Uh-uh."

Her eyebrow raised in puzzlement. "No?"

"No."

"Why?"

"Because I reached my yearly quota of sexual frustration yesterday. Your kisses could drive me crazy, if I'd let them."

She kissed the corners of his mouth, teasing them into a lazy smile. Her hips rocked against his. His eyes danced with the flickering embers of desire. He wanted her, but he was holding back.

"Oh, yeah?" she crooned.

"Yeah. Aren't psychiatrists supposed to be concerned about the mental well-being of their…friends?"

Angelica swiftly realized they were back to the discussion of whether they should be friends or lovers. She could ask for undying love and eternal commitment, or she could follow Hogan's philosophy and take one glorious day at a time, living life to its fullest. She wouldn't cheat herself out of today's pleasures by trying to control what happened in the future, she decided.

She framed Rob's head between her hands. Rather than give him a straight answer, she asked, "Is my wanting to make love with you the source of your stress?''

''No.'' Rob took a deep breath to still the pounding blood in his heart. He knew psychiatrists had a reputation for asking questions and never giving answers. He shifted his weight from one foot to the other. Mentally, he moved off her psychiatrist's couch by doing what he felt certain she would do if he were a patient: he repeated her own question. ''Is your wanting to make love with me the source of your stress?''

''Yes,'' she sighed. ''But this kind of stress isn't bad. It's a motivator.''

''What are you motivated to do to solve your problem?''

Her eyes remained locked with his; her hands dropped to the front of his shirt. Her thumb pushed his top button through its buttonhole; her fingertips caressed the thatch of hair at the V of his collarbones. While one hand touched him, the other hand continued to unfasten the buttons. One tug and his shirttail came loose from his shorts.

An impatient man, Rob had to curb his impulse to push her hands away and quickly undress. He knew exactly how a psychiatrist must feel when he could quickly solve a patient's problem but had to wait for the problem to take care of itself. He sucked his stomach flat as her hands followed the path of his ribs around to the hollow of his spine. One last pull and she completely freed his shirt.

Her hands, gliding over his skin, pausing at each erogenous spot on his torso and slowly circling it, caused a problem he couldn't ignore. Savage need ripped through him. Hard as he tried, he couldn't remain stoically passive.

His arm moved beneath her knees; he lifted her, holding her tightly against his chest as he carried her into the house, into his bedroom. He kissed her passionately, once, then turned and sat down on the bed with her on his lap.

He was an impatient man, but not a simpleton. What they were sharing was too wonderful to spoil by rushing to a greedy, self-indulgent climax. Careless lovers took without giving. He cared for her. He wanted her to experience every thrill possible to woman before he reached the pinnacle of their lovemaking.

"Tell me what pleases you," he whispered, nuzzling, nipping the tender place below her ear.

From the multitude of how-to books she'd read Angelica knew how to please a man, but she'd never given thought to how a man could give her pleasure. She'd never experienced the ultimate heights a woman was supposed to reach. She honestly didn't know where he should touch or what he could do to take her there.

Sexually, she was completely out of touch with herself.

She could pretend, as she had in the past, by moaning and groaning when it seemed appropriate, but she was reluctant to be dishonest with Rob. She'd gone beyond the brink with him. Emotionally, she was committed to him. She loved him. Could she lie to the man she loved? Should she remain silent and commit a lie of omission?

Rob felt the muscles along her spine stiffen, but her fingers continued to make delicious circles around his nipples.

"Talk to me, sweetheart." His hand closed over her fingers. He fell backward against the bed, with her on top of him. "I want to make love *with* you. This is one time your doing all the giving won't satisfy either of us. I can't read your mind. You have to tell me or show me what gives you pleasure."

"Rob, please..." She could satisfy him. Sex was easy for a strong, virile man like Rob.

"Please what?"

She tried to tug her hands free, but failed. "Just... just... let it happen. Th-this isn't the time to talk."

His eyebrows drew together in a dark scowl. Silent lovemaking? he mused skeptically. His thumb moved to the damp palms of her hands. Tenseness? Stammering? Sweating palms? She had all the physical signs of a woman who'd never shared a bed with a man!

Rob bluntly asked, "Are you a virgin?"

"I haven't been confined to a convent for the past thirty years." A nervous twitter of laughter passed through her lips. She fluttered her eyelashes flirtatiously. "Ask me no questions and I'll tell you no lies."

He threaded his fingers between hers, then raised his arms over his head until she was looking him straight in the eye. His legs wrapped around her, securing her against him.

A purely defensive mechanism made Angelica's eyes close.

"Open your eyes, love. I won't let you hide behind laughter or a dark fringe of lashes."

"Let go of me, Rob."

"Why?"

"Because...because..." To bite back the whole unvarnished truth her teeth clamped down on her lower lip.

"You've changed your mind? Do you want to make love with me?"

Her ego cried, *No!* With a whimper of protest, Angelica ceased her struggles and collapsed against him. "Sex isn't what it's cracked up to be, but that doesn't mean it can't be . . . pleasant."

Pleasant? In a flash Rob rolled over until she was on her back, pinned beneath him.

He released her wrists; she flung one arm over her face.

"Angelica, look at me."

Close to tears, she stubbornly refused to let him see her face.

His voice dropped to the intimate level of a soothing caress. He brushed her hair back from her face with his fingers, as he searched for a tactful way to ask very private questions. He had to start at the beginning and proceed slowly.

"Then just listen. I don't know . . . or want to know what has happened between you and another man, unless it affects what happens between us. Do you enjoy holding me?"

She nodded.

He moved to her side, hugging her against him. "Me, too. Sometimes I hug my pillow against me in my sleep. Do you do that?"

For the world, she wouldn't admit she'd gone back into the kitchen and removed the pink flamingo from the top of the refrigerator and held it against her throughout the night. He'd think she was a damned silly female.

She nodded, not trusting herself to keep that secret.

"Of course, you have Figaro. I've thought about getting a pet. A dog, maybe. I always wanted a puppy to lick my face and wag its tail when it saw me."

"Get one."

Angelica felt her muscles slowly relaxing, little by little. Her arm dropped; her hand rested on his shoulder. She hadn't the vaguest idea what he was leading up to, but she was growing blissfully content in his arms.

"Can't. There are pet restrictions at my condo." He watched the strain draining from her face. "What does Figaro do when she wants you to pet her?"

"Brushes up against my legs. Arches her back." A small smile lifted one corner of her mouth as she realized where Rob was leading her. "Sometimes she plops herself on my lap and rubs the side of her face against me when she wants her ears scratched."

"Hmm. Stroking her gives you pleasure?"

"Uh-huh."

"Silent communication. Haven't you ever wished she could talk to you?"

Angelica raised her eyelashes a fraction of an inch. "Yes."

"I wish you'd talk to me." He kissed her forehead, rewarding her for sharing her feelings with him. "I'll get pleasure from knowing where to touch you. You can talk to me. I shouldn't have to guess what you enjoy."

"I like..." She hadn't considered specifically what she liked. Her mind drifted back to the moments of intense pleasure he'd given her. After he knocked her down that first night, she'd swatted at his hands when he was checking her for broken bones, but subconsciously she'd known even then that she liked having him touch her. "I liked having your hands glide over me...as though you were searching for broken bones."

She watched his face, expecting him to laugh at her nonsensical gibberish. He didn't crack a smile.

"Like this?"

His hand moved down her arm, across her slender waist and over her legs.

His casual touch left her longing for something more ardent. "And when you put suntan lotion on me, I liked that."

She'd had fewer clothes on then, he mused. Should he risk removing her top? His hands lightly skimmed beneath the edge of the hem. "Can I take this off?"

Angelica not only agreed, she helped him. She shed more than he'd asked. Only a lacy wedge of underwear separated them when she lay back against the pillow.

"While we were at the beach, did I tell you I wanted to drape your towel around you to keep other male eyes off you?"

"No."

She loved the surge of heat sweeping through her as his eyes hungrily followed the path of his hands as they cupped the undersides of her breasts, then spanned her waist. His large hands made her feel feminine, beautiful.

"I wanted to kiss you . . . here."

He touched the back of her knees.

"I wanted you to touch me...here." Her back arched as she brought his hand to the rosy tip of her breast. "They ached."

The pad of his thumb kissed her, gently urging her nipple to bud into a hard peak. "Like this?"

"Mmm." Her eyes closed; her fingers dug into his forearm. Like a kitten, she arched her back. "Kiss me there?"

The rasp of his shaved cheek against the skin he'd sensitized with his hands sent a shiver of anticipation shimmying to the peaks of her breasts. He complied with more than kisses. His mouth opened, breathing his hot breath across her. With the patience of a saint, he adhered to her request. The dull ache intensified into a raging throb. She wanted to feel him take her into his mouth, but he didn't. He kissed her breasts; but mercilessly, he only did what she told him to do.

When she felt as though they'd surely burst, she leaned forward and whispered into his ear what she longed to have him do.

Rob lightly flicked his tongue over one tip, then the other. "More?" he whispered.

"Much more. Much, much more!"

Nine

———

Through a haze of sensations she heard him murmur, "Lord, woman, who would believe you feel and taste better than you look?"

His strong, long fingers kneaded her taut breasts as his tongue drew the tip deep inside his mouth. Her skin felt afire from the hot moisture of his swirling tongue. An exquisite hunger gnawed at her insides; she drew her knees tightly together to keep it from devouring her. Her bottom squirmed against the sheet, then lifted barely an inch from the mattress. When his hand came to rest on her stomach, her hips arched higher, silently commanding him to touch her inner core.

Rob controlled his inclination to listen to her body language. He pressed a trail of openmouthed kisses in the valley of her breasts. She tasted of sunshine and wildflowers, a heady mixture meant to drive him wild. His tongue danced across to the pouting tip of the breast he'd neglected. His teeth nibbled, his tongue caressed, his hands massaged her. Only his iron will suppressed his own mounting desire.

"Rob, touch me."

"I am, sweetheart."

She moved his hand until his palm lay flat at the apex of her thighs. "Here."

Lacy bikinis and satin skin beckoned him. With one fell swoop he could have her naked beneath him. No. No. No. His own mental command echoed in his ears. He teased the lacy edge with his forefinger. Once, and only once, did his need drive him to dip his finger into the silken curls of her femininity. Maintaining control had its price. He truly didn't know if it was his own palm's moist dampness he felt, or could it possibly be her honeyed sweetness radiating from deep within her that felt wet? He couldn't risk wishful thinking on his part. He couldn't take a chance on rushing her. The heel of his hand slowly rotated against her.

"Oh..." Angelica gasped, her eyes widening to their fullest. Her buttocks clenched in response to the stirrings from within her; her hips writhed beneath his hand. She grabbed his arm to stop the delicious torment. She wanted him to stop; she wanted him to continue for ever. Dizzy from the sensation coursing through her, she didn't know what she wanted.

Deserting the throbbing peaks of her breasts, he lifted his head until he could see her face. Her hands fluttered over his shoulders aimlessly. Her throat worked convulsively, but her lips formed no meaningful words. The signs of escalating passion were obvious. Gently, he peeled off her panties and tossed them aside. His shorts fell to the floor beside them.

"Open your eyes, sweetheart," he coaxed huskily.
The heel of his hand slipped lower as her knees parted
for him. He continued to work his magic on her. "Let
me see the desire burning in them."

She couldn't. Bursts of vivid, vibrant colors painted
the backsides of her eyelids. Explosion after explosion,
each one brighter than the one previous to it. She
mouthed, "Can't. Beautiful. So gloriously beautiful."

When she felt his mouth cover hers, she parted her
lips. Her tongue tangled with his in a ritualistic dance
as old as Adam and Eve. Her arms wound around his
neck as though she were drowning in the tumultuous
waves of sensations he caused.

And then he touched her—really touched her. His
gentle strokes brought her nerve endings from beneath
her skin, exposing them to inconceivable bliss.

"Please, please, please," she chanted in a delirious
frenzy, "come inside of me. Be part of me."

A sweeter invitation Rob had never heard. With all
his heart and soul, he wanted to be part of her. He
couldn't deny her anything when she begged so pret-
tily.

Angelica gloried at his infinitely slow thrust. Her
silky smooth legs wrapped around his waist as she heard
a hiss of air coming from between his lips.

"Angelica, my lovely, adorable Angelica."

He gave to her what he'd asked from her—whispered messages of love and adoration. His voice led her
to new and higher peaks, calling her name, telling her
what he wanted, needed from her.

She responded with a total lack of inhibition. Franti-
cally her lower body twisted, arching beneath his thrust,
plunging, lifting higher. Then her mind shattered into
shards of brilliance, as if she were a piece of invaluable

crystal. Her fingers clutched his buttocks as she fought to stay at the pinnacle, savoring the sensations of her first climax.

Her eyes opened in wonder in time to see Rob's face contort into a mask of ecstasy. His arms were braced, biceps taut as he poured his life's seed into her. He shuddered, completely spent, then lowered himself against her.

Angelica stared at the man she loved, watching his face reveal the change from intense concentration to complete relaxation. A tear of joy slid down her cheek unnoticed. Now she understood what inspired poets and songwriters. Her own ragged heartbeat sang a tune she'd never heard before she'd made love *with* Rob.

Cradled against him, passion sated, her lips touching his cheek, she drifted into a dreamless sleep.

"Sweet dreams?" Rob asked when her eyes lazily opened.

"Why dream when the hero of them is here in my arms?" Smiling, she put her fingers across his lips. "Shh. Don't deny it. You may not think of yourself as a prince or a hero, but to me you are a prince of a man. You saved me from a passionless life, so you must be a hero."

He nibbled on her finger, then kissed it. "If I'm either, it's because of you. You make me feel ten feet tall and richer than Midas."

"I'm just a woman." A woman who loves you beyond reason, she added silently. She wanted to surround him in the glow of her love, not compound his problems by burdening him with her love. "A woman who feels very, very feminine."

Her fingers followed the wrinkle of his brow to the laugh lines radiating from the corners of his eyes.

He caught her wrist, planting a kiss in the palm of her hand. He tried, but he couldn't keep a self-satisfied smile that faintly resembled a cocky grin off his lips. An idea began to formulate in his mind. The more he thought about his idea, the more he liked it.

"What are you thinking?" she asked as his grin grew wider and wider.

He straightened his face. His idea might or might not work out. If it did, he wanted to surprise her.

"Nothing," he lied.

"C'mon, Rob. It's a little late for secrets, isn't it?"

"Speaking of secrets," he said, dropping a kiss on her forehead, then swinging his legs off the bed, "you haven't seen Hogan's paintings."

"Rob!" She stretched the one syllable for all it was worth. "Come back here."

He chuckled, pulling on his shorts. "And let you see that your hero's feet are made of clay? Uh-uh, lady. My recuperative powers aren't unlimited. Once a king, always a king, but once a knight . . ."

"Knight spelled n-i-g-h-t? In case you haven't noticed, it's broad daylight. About noon, I imagine."

He glanced at his wrist, which was bare. "Noon? Definitely time to be up and at 'em. That's not to say I wouldn't mind taking a nap later. Come to think of it, since I am on vacation and I'm supposed to be getting lots of rest, I think we'll have to turn in early, too."

"Morning, afternoon and night? What was that little ditty you recited? 'Once a king . . .'"

He stopped her in midsentence by pouncing on the bed and giving her a loud, smacking kiss.

"Thrice a day keeps the doctor away?" he ad-libbed. Covering his mouth, he gave an exaggerated yawn. "Maybe it's nap time."

Laughing, Angelica pushed him away. He grabbed for her, but she nimbly bounced off the bed. In less time than it took to watch a television commercial, she was dressed—minus her underwear—and inside the closet searching for the secret room.

"My house is a replica of his. Do you think there's a..." She paused when she heard stealthy movement coming from beyond the back of the closet. "You aren't the only one privy to the floor plans of this house. There's somebody in there.

"Maybe the house is haunted by Hogan's ghost?" Rob moved her aside as he reminded himself that he did not believe in the supernatural. If someone was inside the room, there was a logical explanation as to how he or she got there. He pushed against the concealed door. Light spilled through the window overhead.

Stretched out full-length on the work table, using a pink satin pillow for her head, Rob's four-legged nemesis was making herself completely at home.

"Figaro, how did you get in here?" Angelica asked, slipping from behind Rob into the room. Her eyes narrowed. "And what's that underneath your head?"

In silent reply, Figaro rubbed the side of her face against the sleek fabric as if to say, "Mine."

"Oh no, it isn't yours." Two steps closer, she reached for the stuffed flamingo. "Off, cat."

Figaro blinked once, then clumsily swatted at Angelica's hand.

A low rumble of laughter came from directly behind her. She wheeled around. "What are you laughing at? It's your gift she's adopted!"

"Let her have it." The idea that had been formulating in his mind earlier solidified. "I'll get you something better."

Figaro's pointy ears turned directly toward Rob. Her mew sounded as though it had a question mark behind it.

"You'll just have to wait and see, won't you?" Rob replied, ruffling the fur at her nape gently. "The closet door was closed. How did you get in here?"

None too pleased with Figaro's behavior, Angelica squatted to inspect the baseboards. She pointed to the corner of the small room. "Hogan installed a cat door. So that was how she got in earlier, too."

With Figaro in one arm, Rob bent at the waist to help Angelica to her feet. Figaro had the grace to bury her face in shame against his chest. She knew she'd been naughty.

"Don't badger the poor cat. She probably thought I'd brought her a toy."

"No way. She saw me sleeping with it under my head, so..." Her voice dwindled to nothing as she realized what she'd revealed. Her face flamed with embarrassment.

Rob grinned, pulled her against his chest, dropped a kiss on the crown of her head and then turned her toward the easel. Hands full, he whispered, "Take the cloth off the easel. See if you recognize anyone."

As the cloth fell to the floor, Angelica gave a gasp of delight. She moved closer to the painting, instantly recognizing Hogan's jaunty smile and his untied shoelace. She also had no doubts who the young boy was. Rob's hair was lighter, he smiled as though nature had affixed a permanent joke in the back of his mind and he was barefooted, but he was the Rob she had grown to know and love.

"You and Hogan. That must have been the last painting he finished." Her voice shook with emotion.

Tears pooled in her eyes. "He refused to let me take photographs of him. He said my memory would be kinder than a camera." She swallowed hard to clear the lump swelling in her throat. "This is better than a picture."

Rob started to tell her that Hogan hadn't had time to finish it, but didn't. He'd only added the finishing touch. He didn't want credit for Hogan's work.

"Are there any others?"

"Several of Figaro." The cat heard her name mentioned and jumped out of Rob's arms, back to her pillow. Content, she yawned, blinked and shut her eyes. "A few still lifes of what must have been his favorite orchids."

"And one of me. It's hanging in my bedroom."

"I'd like to see it." He lightly pinched the ticklish spot below her ribs to make her look up at him. "And you, too," he mouthed so Figaro couldn't hear.

Without disturbing Figaro's catnap, they left Hogan's secret room. Absorbed in their own private thoughts, both of them were silent as she led the way to her house. Only their fingertips linked them together. For now, it was enough for both of them.

Standing at the foot of her bed, Rob raised her hand to his lips. "I've seen you like that . . . spinning around, with your hair loose, flying around your head like a golden halo."

"He gave it to me when I first moved here. Believe me, I looked like the wrath of God. Fatigue lines under my eyes. Limp, lusterless hair. A permanent twitch." Rob tightened his hold around her waist. "I remember thanking Hogan for the flattering picture. He told me that someday I'd look exactly like the painting."

Rob turned her toward the mirror. His arms draped across her midsection; his thighs touched the backs of her legs. "Look at yourself, Angelica."

She did. Sunlight from the window lit the platinum highlights of her hair. Her cheeks bloomed with a fragile pink that rivaled the color of a cattleya orchid. The worry lines had vanished.

She looked exactly what she was: a woman in love.

Her eyes moved upward to Rob's reflection as her hands skated across his tanned arms. She watched him feather a string of kisses along the side of her neck. His hand stole beneath her cotton top and whispered along her bare skin.

Before her very eyes, she witnessed the instantaneous transformation caused by his light touch. Mesmerized, she watched as his hand cupped the fullness of her breasts. The tips hardened into tight buds; her natural coloring heightened. Her locked knees threatened to buckle. She relaxed against him, willing to let him support her weight.

She helped him in his quest to touch every square inch of her skin by removing the cloth barriers. His raspy groan of appreciation was far from being a polite thankyou, but it served to break her mesmerized state.

He'd made love to her; she'd been an ecstatic recipient. This time, she wanted to give him as much pleasure as he'd given her. Without faking her response, she wanted to please him. She wanted to love him with all her heart and soul.

She squirmed around in his arms until she faced him. "Let me love you," she implored between shy butterfly flicks of her tongue around his flat male nipple. While he hesitated to reply, she kissed generously and sucked gently.

Rob had never been turned on by an aggressive woman. He'd seldom made the singles' cocktail lounge scene for that reason in particular. Just as a woman resented being visually undressed in public, so did a man. Just as a woman didn't like being callously grabbed and groped, neither did he.

But Angelica's caresses were nothing like the bold, mechanical manipulations of a man-hungry woman.

"Your skin smells heavenly," she crooned when she realized his reluctance to let her assume the dominant role. The last thing she'd intended was to threaten his male ego. She brushed her lips against the inside of his arm. "Very masculine."

Her softly spoken praise washed away the taint of brassy women from his tongue. Angelica's special brand of shy seductiveness intrigued him.

Aware of how he enjoyed being held, she pillowed herself against him. He'd shared a privileged piece of information with her. She did the same as she swayed her hips and said, "Dance with me. A slow, slow dance."

Her eyes met his as she hooked her hands at his nape. She leaned backward, secure in his arms. The silent melody of a bluesy song was playing in each of their minds. Her shoulders dipped rhythmically from side to side. As she balanced on one leg, the arch of her other foot climbed up and down the outside of his leg. And still their eyes remained intently locked on each other.

For long minutes, attuned to each other, they shared the same fantasy world.

His slightest touch broadened the dimensions of her expanding love. Her confidence in herself as a woman grew until there were no boundaries restraining her. She touched him, assured by his murmuring there were no confines to restrict her. No place was sacred; no place remained untouched by her lips, teeth and tongue. Each of his sighs gave permission for her to completely have her way with him.

Nothing was impossible.

She felt lighter than a puff of air when he lifted her until her legs circled his waist. She arched upward, feeling as though she could soar. His beloved face was buried into the valley of her breasts. The inner music played on, with a pulsating beat accented by each powerful thrust of his hips. She met the fervent pounding of each note until her entire body tensed. Her climax had the same impact as cymbals crashing together.

But their love song continued.

Long into the lazy afternoon, strains of the melody could be heard coming through his soft whispers and her subdued tones of laughter. Mother Nature provided symphonic background music: the rustle of the wind through the pine trees, the song of a whippoorwill off in the distance and, occasionally, the muted tones of one gator calling to another. All combined, it was a lover's symphony only they could hear.

Tina Lang arrived early for her counseling appointment Monday morning. Angelica spied her pacing back and forth in front of her storefront office before she parked her car in the lot out the back.

"I'm going to pack up the kids and leave Richard," she announced without preliminaries. "He embarrassed the bejesus out of me yesterday at his company picnic. Who the hell does he think he is to call me just a housewife? I may be a housewife, but it takes damned good organizational skills to take care of his kids, keep food on the table and make certain he goes to work wearing a starched shirt. I could teach him a thing or two!''

Angelica unlocked the door and ushered Tina into her office. She listened intently as she fixed a pot of coffee. Like poison, Tina's anger had to be purged from her system.

From previous sessions, she knew Tina had been building up to this outpouring of anger for months. She had been counseling Richard, too, but he was what Angelica called wife-deaf. When he set down his briefcase in the hallway of his home, the earwax started building until he seldom heard a word Tina or the kids said to him.

It was pointless to ask Tina if she had communicated her anger to Richard. He wouldn't have noticed. She wondered if Tina would get his attention if she did leave him. Probably not until he ran out of starched undershorts, Angelica mused, tapping her own sense of humor to keep her emotional equilibrium. Richard's treatment of his wife and children irked her, too.

Angelica had to remind herself of what Tina referred to as the ''superglue'' in her marriage. Love. It bonded Tina and Richard together, making separation impossible. Tina talked about leaving him, but she was only verbalizing her fear of being left behind.

''You should have seen him chatting with his boss's secretary. He probably daydreams about taking over Phil's desk to get Petula as a fringe benefit. I'd be jealous of her if Richard was attracted to her body instead of her brain. He says she is . . . mentally stimulating!'' Tina smacked the flat of her hand with her fist. ''He had the nerve to say it while I was wiping Richie's runny nose. I threw the dirty tissue at him, rounded up the kids and went home.''

Angelica handed Tina a cup of coffee. "You drove home without him."

"He caught the Shoe Sole Express." She saw Angelica's raised eyebrow and explained, "He's too proud to hitch a ride from another employee. He walked home. Didn't you say walking was good for him?"

Several miles under a blistering sun wasn't what Angelica had had in mind when she made that recommendation. "Everything in moderation, Tina."

"It saved an argument. He was too pooped to talk, much less raise his voice, by the time he got home."

"What did he say when he recovered."

"Nothing. He's pouting. As usual, he didn't hear a word I said." Like a windup toy that had wound down, Tina sagged against the corner of Angelica's desk. "I made the biggest mistake of my life the day I fell in love with that power-hungry, overambitious son-of-a-biscuit eater! I ought to leave him."

Angelica blanched as Tina's monologue struck a nerve. Was she making a similar mistake? Would she rue the day she'd fallen for Rob? Disciplined to devote her undivided attention to her patient, Angelica stored that errant thought for later examination.

"What's the worst thing that can happen if you do leave Richard?"

Mulling the question over in her mind, Tina took a gulp of strong coffee. "The kids hating me for depriving them of a father."

"Would you be depriving them of a father?"

"Legally, yes. In reality, no. They barely see him. He's gone in the morning before they get up. He's almost brain-dead when he gets home, so they steer clear of him in the evening."

"How do you feel about that?"

"Guilty. Richard says he wouldn't have to work long hours if it weren't for me and the kids." Tina stared into her cup. "If I leave him, the kids wouldn't just be losing a dad, they'd be losing me, too. I'd have to go back to work."

"Have you considered Richard's idea that you should get a part-time job?"

Tina lifted one shoulder. "I have those builders' business cards you gave me. I telephoned one of them."

"Was he impressed with your qualifications?"

"With my diploma I'm overqualified. Interior decorators without diplomas are a dime a dozen. Builders cut corners by hiring them to keep their costs low."

Angelica mentally backtracked to one of Tina's earlier sessions. "Didn't you tell me a good decorator could save their clients money?"

"Yes."

"Can't you work on a commission basis?"

"Maybe," Tina hedged. Her eyes darted around the office as she tried to avoid giving a direct answer. The silence became unbearable. "I used to be a good decorator, but I've been out of touch with the commercial world. My business contacts are nonexistent. What if I couldn't make enough commissions to pay a housekeeper?"

"That's a risk you'd have to take." Angelica leaned forward in her chair. "Tina, are you selling yourself short? You said you loved the job you had before you married. Are you letting what Richard says affect your sense of self-worth?"

With a deep sigh Tina deposited her cup on Angelica's desk. "I hate being a clinging vine, hanging on to Richard. But...what if I get a job and fail? Won't that prove I *am* just a housewife?"

"You won't fail, Tina. As long as you keep your family and your job in their proper perspective, you'll be fine."

"Maybe getting out in the business world would help my marriage. I'd have something more exciting to discuss with Richard during dinner than the price of the groceries on his plate." A small smile tugged at her lips. "Maybe the kids would get over their case of being mama-deaf if I'm not yammering at them day and night."

Angelica rose and circled her desk. She hugged Tina. It had been a long haul getting Tina to risk stepping forward. She continued to have a bad case of the "maybes," but at least she'd put her anger aside. She appeared willing to move off dead center in a positive direction.

In her next session with Richard, Angelica would strive to get him to slow down his work pace so he could catch up with his family. If he didn't, eventually he'd kill Tina's love—superglue could only withstand a certain amount of constant friction. Unless Richard changed his attitude, Tina would mentally outgrow him.

"I'm going straight home to change into interior decorator glad rags." Tina strode purposefully toward the door. "Then I'm going to personally contact several builders."

"Call me if I can be of help. Otherwise I'll see you next Monday to hear about your interviews."

"Will you keep an opening for me in case I'm working during the morning hours?"

Angelica walked Tina to the door. "I'm always available if you need me."

As she watched Tina cross the street, she pondered the similarities between Richard and Rob. Aside from both of their names starting with the same letter, they had many personality traits in common. Rob's attitude had changed.

But had his attitude really changed, she asked herself, or had his circumstances changed? A man on vacation could drop his corporate image. What would happen when Rob returned to his job?

Angelica twisted a lock of hair around her thumb and began rubbing it between her fingers. Catching herself in her old worry habit, she uncurled her hair from her index finger.

"I will not worry about his future. I can't hold back the hands on the clock. Deal with the here and now!"

She'd left Rob sound asleep. Blueberry muffins, bran flakes and a happy mug filled with positive thoughts written on strips of paper were on the breakfast table. Would he take the hint?

Glancing at the sky, she guessed at the time of day. Tenish, she calculated. He'd be awake. She moved to the telephone on her desk, picked up the receiver and dialed her home number.

She waited and waited. "No answer. He may have gone over to his house." She dialed Hogan's old number.

On the second ring, Rob picked up the phone. "Emery residence."

"Hi, Rob. How'd you like the muffins?"

"I wondered why you left an empty plate on the table. In TV commercials the kids eat bran flakes out of bowls," he teased.

Angelica groaned. "Figaro ate them. She's going to be the size of a barn if I continue baking for you."

"Do cats get gout?"

"Only when they drink beer," she replied, grinning at a mental picture of Figaro with one fat paw, gobbling baked goods. "What are the two of you planning to do while I'm at work?"

"Working out how to free the gators. I've made a couple of phone calls to the hatcheries. They recommended I hire Abe Grant to collect the eggs. I spoke to him and he was willing to harvest the eggs, but couldn't feed the gators. He said he'd find someone to feed them."

Angelica nodded. Abe Grant's reputation for handling alligators was widespread. "Did you ask about releasing the gators?"

"I mentioned it. He said poachers would be thick as thieves around the area if word got out. I guess this is going to have to be a hush-hush operation." Rob chuckled. "I'll have to buy a gross of firecrackers."

"Don't worry. I learned my lesson. I'll lock the doors and call the sheriff."

"I'm kind of glad you weren't sensible the night I arrived. One look at you and the earth shook while fireworks exploded."

"Flattery? Careful, Rob. I might start to believe that silver tongue of yours."

"Advertising executives are allowed to stretch the truth a tiny bit."

"Mmm." Angelica glanced at her appointment book. "I'd like to invite you to lunch, but I'm running a tight schedule today."

Rob made a tsking noise. "Aren't you the lady who preaches good times and relaxation?"

"Mondays are busy. I'll be home by five, though."

"I'll fix steaks."

Angelica heard him say something while muffling the phone with his palm. "What did you say?"

"Figaro's ears shot up like TV antennas. I threatened her with bodily harm. I won't tell you what she did."

"Why not?"

"Because you'd think I was making it up. While we filmed the cat food commercial I was around dozens of cats. Not one of them could do what she just did. Loudly, I might add. I remember an award-winning commercial where a bunch of children were in a Japanese hot tub—"

Angelica grinned. "Too much sugar in her diet. It causes bubbles in her stomach. Don't plan any commercials starring Figaro."

"Did you know she's cross-eyed?" Rob asked in a low whisper, not wanting to offend Figaro for a second time.

"Of course I know. That's why she's uncoordinated. It's part of her charm."

"Stop it, Figaro!" He didn't bother to cover the phone. "Don't eavesdrop and you won't be offended. Sweetheart, I'm going to have to toss Figaro outside. Hurry home. Bye."

"Hurry home," she repeated after she'd returned the phone to its cradle. They had to be two of the sweetest words in the English language. She wrote them on a strip of paper to put in her happiness mug.

Ten

Rob's hand rested on the telephone as he gave it a hard look. His goodbye should have been prefaced with "Love you," he mused. Next time it would be. He raised his hand the same instant the telephone rang. He grinned. Maybe Angelica had the same idea! Or maybe she'd developed a sixth sense about him and knew he needed to hear those words.

Without a second thought, he picked up the phone and said, "I love you, too."

He expected to hear the soft sound of pleasure; he heard a gasp, then a burst of laughter.

"That's nice, boss. Should I book my cruise for two instead of one?" Olivia asked.

"Olivia?" Caught off guard and slightly embarrassed, he asked abruptly, "Why are you calling?"

"Well," she teased, drawing the word out to the limits, "I knew you'd be missing me terribly, so—"

"Olivia, cut the comedy."

"Yes, sir! I just booked you on a flight to New York. You leave Orlando—"

"What?"

"I said—"

"I heard what you said." Shifting mental gears from leisure to business, he said decisively, "Forget it. My two week vacation has barely started."

"Not from the way you answered your phone," Olivia muttered. Then in a brisk tone she replied, "It's been cut short. Earl wants you here, pronto."

Rob fervently shook his head. Figaro jumped onto his lap, licked his face and began purring.

"You're booked on the one o'clock flight."

"Cancel it."

"It's a nonrefundable ticket."

"I'll reimburse the company out of my pocket."

"C'mon, Rob," Olivia implored. She'd worked for him long enough to know exactly how to handle her boss when he was being stubborn. "Do you want Lombardo to get the job?" Competition. "This isn't a mail-in multiple choice test you're going to be given." Challenge. "Pack your bags and haul your butt up here." Direct order. And if none of those worked— guilt. "You owe Earl at least that courtesy for all he's done for you."

Rob sucked his lower lip between his teeth as he listened to Olivia. He didn't want Lombardo to get his job, and he didn't want to thwart Earl. But he sure as hell didn't want to leave Angelica!

He glanced at his wrist. His watch was on the dresser in the bedroom. "What time is it?"

"Twelve minutes after ten."

"It's an hour from here to the airport."

"You have plenty of time," Olivia assured him.

Rob felt his stomach knot. Why did he have the distinct feeling he was sitting in the top part of an hourglass and the sands were funneling out from under him? Worse, why did he have the feeling he was running out on Angelica? He couldn't leave without at least talking to her.

"I can't possibly make the afternoon flight."

There was dead silence on the other end, as if Olivia had put her hand over the mouthpiece, and then a shuffle, as if she were passing it over.

"What the hell do you mean, you can't get back here?" Earl roared. "Goddammit, man, opportunity is knocking at your door!"

Rob groaned when he heard the cliché. Through tight lips, he said, "I'll be there. Tomorrow."

Figaro gave him a cross-eyed glare. Her front paw took a swipe at the spot on his cheek she'd licked, but missed. Rob's arm instantly crooked around her midsection to keep her from falling off his lap.

"Early. You're scheduled with the shrink at eight o'clock. I want to give you a pep talk before you see her."

The knot in Rob's stomach twisted tighter than a hangman's noose. "I said I'll be there."

Figaro squirmed in his arms until he released her.

"I'll have Olivia arrange for a later flight. See you soon."

He heard the phone changing hands again as Earl said, "I knew I could count on him."

Rob threaded his fingers through his hair. He had to have time to talk to Angelica, to make her understand why he agreed to abruptly end their time together.

"Make reservations on the latest flight out of Orlando."

"That's a midnight flight, with a lengthy layover in Atlanta. You won't be in New York until six tomorrow morning."

"I don't care if I have to go directly from the airport to the office. Book it!"

"Okay, okay! Don't bite my head off! You'll fly on the usual carrier. Pick your ticket up at the airport." Her eyes twinkled mischievously as she said, "Love ya'!" and disconnected the line.

Rob immediately dialed the operator to get Angelica's office phone number. Reciting it, he punched in the numbers. He dreaded breaking the bad news to her. How would she react? Would she grab for a notepad and jot down her feelings, then shred them?

He hated the thought of her being angry with him. Mentally, he began justifying his decision to leave. She'd known all along he planned on returning to New York. He had a job there. His future was there. He realized now that discussing his future plans must have become a taboo subject. She hadn't brought up the subject and neither had he. But subconsciously, both of them had realized he would be leaving her.

"Busy! Damn!"

She'd said they couldn't have lunch together because she had a tight schedule on Mondays. Unsettled, frustrated, he rose and began pacing the length of the room. A profusion of thoughts jumbled in his mind. Selfishly, he considered asking her to drop everything and come with him. Certain she'd refuse him, he rejected that idea. Angelica wouldn't abandon her responsibilities to her patients, much less the gators and orchids. She'd made a choice when she moved from the city to the house next door to Hogan. Much as he disliked admitting it, he empathized with her decision. She belonged here.

He also realized he didn't fit into Angelica's or Hogan's shoes. Yes, he'd let his wing-tipped shoes pinch his toes by letting the stress of his job get to him, but thanks to her help he'd now be able to cope with that stress.

He couldn't turn his back on everything he'd busted his ass to achieve. Could he?

Rob shook his head. Angelica wouldn't expect that of him.

His head snapped up toward the ceiling. He loved Angelica; he loved his job. Those were the only truths, and they weren't compatible. What he didn't know for certain was what she expected of him and how much either of them was willing to sacrifice.

He had to talk to her!

He picked up the phone and tried again. His heart skipped a beat when it rang. "Be there, Angelica. Be there!"

"Dr. Franklin speaking."

Her voice sounded brisk, somewhat distracted. "It's me, Rob."

Smiling, she closed the family history file she'd been updating. "Hi."

"Are you with a patient?"

"Not yet, but I'm expecting one any minute." Curious as to why he'd called twice within the hour, she asked, "What can I do for you?"

"Are you certain you can't make it for lunch? I have something important to discuss."

"Rob, I'd love to, but I can't."

"Business before pleasure?" In a conciliatory voice, he added, "I understand." He fervently hoped she would. "My secretary called."

"Oh?"

Unable to think of a means to soften the blow, he said, "I'm booked on the midnight flight to New York City. The tests start tomorrow."

Angelica slumped back in her chair as though the wind had been knocked from her. "Midnight?" she managed to squeak.

"Yeah. I want you to know Olivia booked me on an earlier flight, but I refused. It wasn't until Earl, my mentor, got on the phone that I agreed to return to work."

Beg him to stay, her id shrieked; he's loyal to his job, her superego countered. Somewhere in the middle of the two extremes, she whispered, "I'll miss you. Don't worry about the farm. Abe and I can manage it."

Ask me to stay, he silently ordered, rubbing his forehead. When the pause became unbearable, he said, "Will you come with me?"

She was tempted. Lord, she was tempted. Sanity prevailed. She couldn't uproot herself. She had patients with major problems. Her conscience would plague her if she permanently hung a closed sign on her office door.

"Maybe I'll get up there during my vacation," she replied, praying his invitation extended that far into the future.

"When is that?"

"Christmas."

Rob groaned. "My scheduled vacation is at Thanksgiving. What the hell are we going to do? I can't stay and I don't want to leave."

She tried to think of consoling words, but a web of self-pity shrouded her mind. She'd counted on his being with her at least ten more days. Dammit, it wasn't fair! She falls in love with a man and while she's basking in the warmth of the newness of her love, the sun sets and he flies north. A tear slid from the corner of her eye. Don't be a bawl baby until after he leaves, she chastised. Be it two hours, two days or two weeks, his departure won't be a damned bit easier.

"I'll write," she promised.

"I'm a lousy correspondent. I'll call you. We still have until midnight. Maybe we can come up with a solution."

His ounce of hope submerged in her pool of despair. Tonight was all they had. She had to hold herself together until he boarded the airplane.

"Hurry home, love."

Angelica blinked her eyes. The tinkling of the bell on her door warned her that her next patient had arrived. "I will."

She hung up, pasted a fake smile on her face and rose to stand behind her desk. It wasn't her patient waiting for her, but a police officer.

"Dr. Franklin, we've got an emergency at the hospital. One of your patients, Shelly Cates. She wrapped her car around a tree. Her mother thinks it may have been intentional."

Automatically Angelica reached for her purse, switched on the recording device on her telephone and pushed her personal problems into the background. Without a moment's hesitation, she rushed toward the door, knowing what to expect. She worked with the entire family. There was no doubt in her mind that Mrs. Cates would be an emotional basket case if she thought her only child had tried to take her life. She hung the Emergency sign on the office door and ran to her car.

Hours later, she stepped into a telephone booth at the hospital and dialed Rob's number.

Without social preliminaries, she said, "Rob, I'm at the hospital with a patient. From the looks of things, I'm going to have to stay with her parents until their daughter is out of the operating room."

"How long?"

She hadn't cried over Rob's departure, but the thought of Shelly's not making it through surgery had tears cascading down her face. "I don't know. It's bad, Rob. Her parents are blaming each other and themselves. Her father bought her the car for her sixteenth birthday. She had an argument with her mother and took off in it. Five minutes later, she hit a telephone pole. I have to stay here in case she doesn't make it. They need me."

I need you! He bit his lip to keep from blurting out the words. He could tell from the drone of her voice that she was emotionally exhausted. She needed his support, not recriminations.

"Is there anything I can do?"

"Pray."

"I will, Angelica."

"Mrs. Cates is coming down the corridor. I'm going to have to go, Rob." How absolutely bizarre that she'd be saying that to him. He was the one who had to go.

"I'll call you from New York."

"Bye." As she reached to put the phone on the hook, she thought she heard "I love you." She put the receiver back to her ear, but heard only the dial tone. She must have been thinking the words so loudly she thought she'd heard them.

* * *

"Good to have you back where you belong, Rob."
Earl clapped Rob on the back exuberantly. "Sorry to
cut your vacation short, but I know you must have been
going stir-crazy stretched out on the beach with nothing to occupy your mind besides worrying about your
promotion."

Tight-lipped, Rob mutely cursed the abrupt end of his
stay at Hogan's house. The red-eye flight he'd taken
back to New York was appropriately named. He felt as
though Figaro had scratched kitty litter in his eyes.

"Lockey's arranging for the psychiatrist to begin
working up your profile was a break for us." Earl
chuckled and squeezed his protégé's shoulder. In a low
confidential tone, he said, "Stearnes couldn't get hold
of Mike Lombardo. I'd say you're a lucky son of a
bitch."

"Yeah, lucky," Rob grumbled.

He'd finally left a hastily scrawled note for Angelica. She still hadn't gotten back when he'd left at ten
the previous evening. He could only assume she was still
at the hospital. He felt like the lowest scum on earth for
leaving without talking, face-to-face, to her. She had to
be disappointed in him. He was disappointed in himself.

"I can't wait for you to meet Lockey's shrink. It
doesn't take a mental giant to figure out why he was so
determined to hire her as a consultant. She's gorgeous!
You'd think a man his age, with heart problems and al-
imony payments to three ex-wives, would have better
sense."

Rob clamped his mouth shut to hold back his opinion. His stomach churned at the thought of being a
pawn in Lockey's dating game. His lips hardly moved

as he asked, "When do I get the privilege of meeting her?"

"Any time you're ready." Earl gave him a once-over. He dug deep into his pocket, then dangled a chrome-plated key under Rob's nose. "Here's my key to the executive men's room. You'd better make use of my electric razor."

Realizing Earl expected him to be thrilled by the magnanimity of his gesture, Rob forced a stiff smile to his lips. "Thanks. If you'll pardon me, I'll collect my spare set of clothes from my office before I clean up."

"Have Olivia call Lockey's office when you're ready. His secretary will notify his new honey bunch that you're ready, willing and able to bedazzle her with your brilliance."

Rob crossed to the door with his hand pressed to his stomach. The airline's coffee and Olivia's brew were battling for supremacy. He'd have given Earl's key to the men's bathroom for one of Angelica's blueberry muffins.

Mentally, he kicked himself across the span between the two offices. He shook his head and wondered just what the hell he was doing here.

Angelica snared the pillow close to her chest. She inhaled Rob's scent back to the far recesses of her subconscious where unfulfilled desires were stored, where time and distance were irrelevant.

In her sleep, she smiled as Rob gave her a sexy wink, then kissed her. He swirled her around and around, until she was dizzy.

Hurry home . . . hurry home . . . hurry home.

Rob's laughter filled the pauses as he began jogging away from her. She tried to run, but her arms were filled with happy mugs, pads of paper, boxes of cereal and paintbrushes. Figaro kept weaving figure eights around her feet.

"Where are you, Rob?" she mumbled, her eyelids fluttering as she searched for him.

Her legs pumped up and down, but she wasn't getting anywhere. Faster, her id screamed. I want him!

Her breathing grew shallow. Her pulse raced. A blur of green grabbed her, slowing her to a snail's pace. Her heart pounded as though it were about to shatter into a million pieces, when a black chasm yawned in front of her.

She had to reach him before he disappeared inside it!

"Rob! Stop! Let me help you!"

Angelica sat bolt upright in bed. Her cry echoed in the sultry air. She dug the heels of her hands into her eyes to stop the flow of tears running down her cheeks. Her heart continued to pound heavily.

"It's only a nightmare," she whispered. "Only your subconscious playing vile tricks on you."

Figaro moved off her feet and up the length of her legs as though she knew her mistress needed comfort.

"I'm okay, Figaro. Honest." She wiped her face on the sleeve of her nightgown. The familiar feel of Figaro's silky fur and the sound of her purring consoled Angelica. "I didn't mean to scare you."

She cuddled Figaro against the curve of her body as she rolled to her side and glanced toward the window. Almost dawn, she thought. His flight should have arrived. She wondered if he'd be making his way to his apartment or heading straight for the office. His note had left out the specific arrangements that had been made for him.

"His note said he'd call me the minute he arrived to explain what happened," she confided, pressing her lips against the crown of Figaro's head. "He will. The phone will ring. I'll answer it, and..."

He'll sound exactly like Richard Lang: curt and harried.

She pinched her lips together tightly as the pleasant daydream she'd been about to weave was pierced by a shaft of reality. Daydreams could be infinitely more pleasurable than nightmares, but neither dealt with facts. Like it or not, she had to face the situation. Rob had been summoned; he'd departed.

Sure, he'd call. Rob had unfinished business in Florida—the gator farm. He'd be contrite; he'd apologize. He'd politely issue another invitation for her to join him in New York. When she refused, he might have his secretary send a dozen roses to pacify her. But she had to accept the truth. The days of flamingos and sand castles were gone. She'd known from the time of his first kiss that the sunny days and torrid nights would come to an end.

Between Rob's departure and Shelly's accident—it was an accident; Shelly's car had hit an oil slick—yesterday had been the kind of day that made a person want to tear it off the calendar to keep from being reminded of it. She'd had to hide her tears from Mr. and Mrs. Cates. Now they gathered in her eyes. She didn't stifle them behind a stiff upper lip as she had before she'd gone to bed. She needed a good crying jag. Tears were the mind's antiseptic. She'd been hurt by Rob's hasty departure. To keep the pain from turning into hateful bitterness, she let her tears flow freely.

She cried harder than she had the day Hogan died, but not because she had loved the old man less than his nephew. Hogan had believed he was departing on another grand adventure; Rob was going back into the same hell he'd left. Each tear she shed for Rob was a watery testimonial for what could have been, what ought to have been a lasting kind of love. Clinging to Figaro for solace, she cried as though her heart were broken.

Sorrowful minutes later, she gulped a quieting breath into her lungs. "I'm gonna miss him, Figaro."

On hearing her name, Figaro mewed.

"Yeah. I know, kitty." She sniffed. She rubbed the cat's tummy until Figaro curled her tail around her body and began to purr. "You are, too. But we'll manage. You'll have to do without filching his breakfast and I'll have to do without his sweet loving, but we'll cope. I promise you, the sun will still rise. Tonight the stars will come out and the moon will shine. The earth doesn't revolve around Rob Emery."

A private corner of her world would always revolve around Rob, but she wouldn't admit it aloud for Figaro to hear. She knew without a doubt her inner clock was set to awaken with his good-morning kiss. She'd go to bed at night listening to a lover's tune played on the clock radio inside her head.

She loved Rob Emery. He'd gone, but that didn't stop the loving any more than her tears were able to stop the dull ache in her heart.

Rob left the executive bathroom with three pieces of tissue clinging to his face where he'd nicked himself shaving. He'd had one hell of a time looking in the mirror without rushing into one of the stalls to relieve his queasy stomach of its contents.

He had to keep his promise to call Angelica, but he didn't know what to say. In her book, the words *I'm sorry* covered a multitude of sins. She'd accept his apology and be willing to go on from there.

But where? he wondered. The moment he'd locked up her house he'd known he wanted her with him. He positively dreaded the thought of going back to his empty apartment after work. But at gut level, he knew she didn't belong in the big city any more than Hogan's gators belonged in the Bronx Zoo.

He strode down the corridor on his way to the elevator, glancing at the nameplates beside the closed walnut doors. Earl had a working office on the same floor as Rob's office, but up here Earl had another suite of offices, to impress prospective clients. Rob hesitated, then stopped in front of the door that led into the offices of the soon-to-be-appointed vice president.

Automatically, he twisted the gold-plated knob. The door swung open on its hinges. He should have felt the thrill of anticipation when he saw the inch-thick, cream-colored carpet, the costly antique receptionist's desk, the one-of-a-kind lithograph prints neatly hanging on the wall.

He felt physically ill.

His curiosity should have urged his feet forward. His fingertips should have itched with desire to touch the rich brocade fabric covering the sofa and chairs clustered together at one side of the room. He should have been forming a mental picture of going beyond the waiting room, into the office.

He remained statuelike in the hallway. His imagination only extended itself to wondering how the carpet would feel beneath his bare feet. Somehow he knew it would give him the same tactile pleasure as blades of grass.

Dammit, Angelica, I don't belong on Hogan's gator farm. This is where I've groomed myself to be! Why do I feel as though I'm standing inside a chrome-and-steel tomb, watching my own funeral? I should be exhilarated, charged with dynamic energy!

He tilted his head to one side, waiting for her melodic voice to gently guide him toward self-realization.

Silence. Cold, sterile silence was the only thing he heard until the elevator bell softly chimed. He backed away from the open door. Sluggishly, he shuffled toward the parting stainless steel doors.

His stomach sank to his toes as the elevator swiftly dropped to the floor below. He straightened his tie and tugged on the immaculate French cuffs that extended exactly one-quarter inch below the cuff of his pin-striped suit. Old habits die hard, he mused. Once I'm back in the swim of things, I'll feel better.

Olivia grinned at him as he strode into his office.

"Hey, you're looking sharp. Have you heard the latest news on the office grapevine?"

Rob shook his head, then clasped his hand to the back of his neck to ease the pounding sensation.

"Mike Lombardo refused to cut his vacation short. You know what that means, don't you?"

"Yeah." He's smarter than I am, he added silently. He bent over her desk and scooped a notepad and pencil into his hands. "Olivia, call the florist and have a couple of dozen roses sent to this address, would you?"

She glanced at the name and address, mildly curious. "What do you want written on the card? The usual polite don't-call-me-I'll-call-you brush-off?"

Rob shifted his weight to one foot; his fingers plowed through his dark hair. His head felt as though it would split apart.

"On second thought," he murmured softly, his eyes lighting up as inspiration hit. "Don't order flowers. I'll take care of this personally."

He loosened his tie, unfastened his collar button and shrugged out of his suit jacket. Carelessly, he tossed his jacket onto the back of a chair, then rolled up his cuffs.

"Don't you have an appointment with the psychiatrist?" Olivia asked, slightly appalled by Rob's behavior. "You can't go in there looking like that."

"Can't I?" Rob replied, grinning. "Sit back and watch me."

"That's crazy! She'll have the little men wearing white coats come and get you! Do you want to spend your life weaving straw baskets at a funny farm?"

Rob braced one arm on Olivia's desk; he rapped his chest with one knuckle right above his heart, then pointed to his temple. "It's what's inside here and here that counts. If the real me isn't what Lockey, Stearnes and Cordell want, then that's their loss."

Eyes round, she watched him stride toward the door. "I'll call and tell her you're on your way up there."

"You do that. And while you're on the phone, book me a reservation on the noon flight to Orlando. Have a rental car ready and waiting. No, make that a pickup truck if they have one."

"But Rob, your sessions are supposed to last all week!"

Rob chuckled. "Trust me, Olivia. This interview won't last long."

* * *

Angelica steered around the potholes in the lane

weaving through the scrub oaks and pines. Her foot pushed harder against the accelerator the closer she came to her house. Thin wisps of grayish smoke spiraled around her car.

Brush fires weren't untypical this time of the year. Rain was always short, and this area was the lightning capital of the world. It was a dangerous combination.

She gripped the steering wheel with white knuckles as the right front tire hit a hole. "The whole damned day has been littered with disasters," she gritted between clenched teeth.

Rob hadn't bothered to call. Figaro had devoured an entire box of bran flakes. The wildlife department had notified her that she'd be risking a fine if she removed the fence around the alligator ponds. And now her house was burning to the ground. The only bright spot in her day had been Tina's call to tell her she'd gotten a job. Otherwise, from start to finish, this was a day of infamy!

The wheel lurched to the right, hard. She fought for control as she heard a whoosh of air, then saw the front of the car sag. She applied the brake, simultaneously turning the air blue with a string of curses.

She switched off the ignition, grabbed her purse and leaped out of the car. Shaking beyond measurement on a Richter scale, she kicked the good front tire.

"Why don't you go flat, too!"

She was halfway between the highway and the house, and had to decide which way to go. She stepped out of her high heels and jogged toward the house. She wasn't a woman who'd run away from a problem.

She noticed the smoke appeared to be getting thinner the closer she came to the house. That didn't make sense. Fires didn't put themselves out.

Rounding the bend at a full gallop, she spotted an unfamiliar truck parked in front of her house, and decided that Abe Grant must have arrived to feed the gators. Her steps slowed to a trot. Abe must have extinguished the fire. She paused, bending at the waist as she gasped huge gulps of air. Her fingers kneaded the sharp pain in her side.

The day wasn't a total disaster, she thought, immensely glad her house hadn't burned to the ground.

She straightened, sniffing the air. Unless her nose had gone haywire she could almost swear she smelled beef being cooked.

"Just a figment of your imagination," she chided softly, but hope made her heart thud in her chest. How many times in the past thirty-six hours have you had the same sensation when you heard the phone ring? she berated herself. He hasn't given you a second thought since he hopped on the airplane.

In spite of the mental pep talks she'd given herself between disasters throughout the day, the initial hurt she'd felt had gradually been tainted by anger. She'd written his name over and over on a sheet of paper, then shredded it. As the confetti slid through her fingers, her fury had increased in proportion.

She sniffed again. Wishful thinking didn't have the same odor as steaks fixed on an open grill! Her eyes narrowed. If Mr. Love-'em-and-Leave-'em thought he could waltz in and out of her life when the whim struck him, he had another think coming!

* * *

Stretched out on a chaise longue, with Figaro purring on his chest, Rob closed his red-rimmed eyes. To say he'd merely charred the first batch of steaks would be minimizing reality, he mused, opening one scratchy eyelid. The flames had been three feet tall when Figaro had boxed his ears. It was a wonder he hadn't burned the place down around both of them the way the sparks had been flying. He'd drained his last ounce of energy stomping out the grass fire around the grill.

It felt good to be home. The steaks were sizzling on the grill. Champagne was chilled in the ice bucket. And the wacky gift he'd bought at the airport had been wrapped and hidden under a lilac bush. Soon his sweet, sweet Angelica would be home, and everything would be right in his world.

Angelica silently stalked toward the man reposed on the chaise longue. A major war battled inside her head. One part of her wanted to bean him with her purse; the other wanted to throw her arms around his neck and give him a mighty hug. She wanted to jump up and down, screaming and shouting at him; she wanted to whisper sweet nothings in his ear. She wanted to kick him off her property; she wanted him to stay as long as he could.

Her last thought stuck in her mind. How long could he stay? No, no, she corrected, not could...would. When the big boss in New York snapped his fingers, would he sprout wings again?

Figaro stirred, turning her head toward Angelica and meowing a greeting.

"Shh, Figaro." Rob scratched behind her ears to make her stay with him. "The steaks are doing fine. I fixed one for you, too."

"Me, three?" Angelica asked, deciding she wouldn't boot him off the property... yet.

Rob grinned, lazily rolling to his side. "You're number one."

Silver-tongued devil. In her present frame of mind, flattery would earn him a swift kick on the backside. She tried valiantly to ignore his eyes as they appreciatively caressed her through her daffodil-yellow shirt-waist dress. Her knees felt weak, so she folded her legs and sat Indian style a good ten feet away from him. She knew the closer she came the more tempted she'd be to let sanity fly out the back door of her mind as desire knocked on the front door.

"You have every right to be mad as hell," Rob said, assessing the rigid stiffness of her back, knowing she desperately needed a pad of paper or a pencil to break. He'd planned on making a joke about not wearing a watch and being a little late, but he didn't think she'd laugh.

"I am."

"Would a humble apology get me back in your good graces?"

"No."

"I'm perfectly willing to grovel on hands and knees."

His audacity automatically made her lips twitch with a fleeting smile. Uh-uh, she wouldn't let him get around her by tickling her funny bone.

"You aren't going to make this easy, are you?"

"No." She'd been easygoing the last time he was here. Look what that had gotten her—tears and heartache.

Rob picked Figaro up behind her front legs and looked straight into her crossed eyes. "And I accused you of being clumsy," he muttered. "I'm the bumbling idiot."

Angelica refrained from agreeing with him. "How long will you be here this time?" she asked, going straight for the jugular vein. "Two days? Two weeks?"

"Tomorrow." The way her face crumpled gave him the courage to venture, "All our tomorrows, if you'll marry me."

"Marry you?" she repeated, stunned.

Speaking to Figaro, he said, "Maybe I should have plied her with wine and given her the present first. What do you think?"

Figaro put her paw on his lips.

"Shut up?" he asked, the words muffled in cat fur.

Angelica's knees were definitely too weak to support her in an upright position now. On all fours and none too gracefully, she crawled toward the chaise longue. "Figaro, if you want muffin for breakfast, get your foot out of his mouth."

Jumping off Rob's lap, Figaro ran toward the lilac bush.

Rob dropped off the chaise to his knees. His arms opened just as Angelica's knee caught in the hem of her skirt. She pitched forward, knocking Rob flat on his back, with her nose squashed against his chest.

"Are you hurt?" Rob asked when she didn't move.

"No."

"Dammit, woman." He clamped his hands on her trembling shoulders. He couldn't tell if she was laughing or crying. "Look at me."

"Can't."

"You can and will."

Her head bobbed up. A chorus of laughter bubbled through her lips as their love song trumpeted in her ears. He wanted to marry her! Her ears were ringing, but it wasn't from practically knocking herself senseless. Rob Emery wanted to marry her!

"Yes, I can and will," she repeated in typical psychiatrist fashion to let him know she'd heard every wonderful word he'd said. "But first, you've got to tell me what happened in New York."

"First things first," he agreed wholeheartedly.

Rolling over until she was pinned beneath him, he kissed her with all the love he felt for her. "I love you, Angelica Franklin. I made one hell of a mistake leaving here without telling you."

Between kisses, she murmured, "You promised you'd call. I almost suffocated, holding my breath while I waited to hear from you."

He fanned her hair out from around her face. "I didn't want to tell you I love you long distance. I wanted you right where you are in case you needed convincing that you love me."

"I told you I was falling in love with you."

"And never mentioned it again, not even while we made love."

"I told you." She placed his hand on her heart. "You must not have heard me."

"I need the words, Angelica."

"I love you, Rob Emery... beloved nephew of Hogan Potter...prince of my heart...and definitely a hero. I love you." She punctuated each phrase with a fervent kiss. "I'll even make the grand sacrifice to marry you."

"What's that?"

"I'll move to New York."

Rob chuckled. "I don't think that will be necessary. I think I shocked the psychiatrist."

"Oh, yeah?"

"She took one look at my open-necked white shirt and my rolled-up sleeves and began scribbling in her notebook. And that was only the beginning of the interview. Her steno pad was brimming with my utterly truthful answers to her questions.''

''You purposely led her to believe—''

''That I didn't give a damn what she wrote in her little notebook? Yep. She tried to keep a straight face while I told her what the inkblots represented, but I'm fairly certain I horrified her. All I could see in them was you—your face, your smile, the way your hair curls. She knows I'm completely obsessed with the thought of you. Believe me, you don't have to worry about Lockey, Stearnes and Cordell. I'll be lucky if they're willing to give me a decent reference.''

''Rob, you shouldn't have messed up your chances for me.'' Guilty feelings reared their ugly heads. ''In six months you'll hate me for ruining your career.''

''In six months I'll have another job in advertising. Only I'll make certain I'm not working a sixty-hour week to keep it.'' When she shook her head, he trapped it between his hands. ''I didn't flub the test for your sake, I did it for me. It took me less than half an hour inside the Cordell Building to realize I'd been existing on adrenaline for months. The one and only fear I had was that you wouldn't want an unemployed executive with no prospects on the horizon.''

''Does that worry you?''

''No. I have a healthy bank balance. Lord knows I haven't had time to spend the salary I earned. I can always expand the gator farm if we run out of steaks and wine.'' He cocked his head toward the grill. ''Speaking of steaks, I think I'd better check on them. How do you like yours?''

Angelica nipped playfully at his finger. ''Raw.''

''Starving, huh?''

"No, just eager to get on to bigger and better things."

"We could skip dinner," he suggested, standing up and pulling her with him. "Figaro won't mind eating a couple of extra steaks."

"You're spoiling her."

"Uh-uh. It's you I plan on spoiling." He wrapped his arm around her waist, unwilling to completely let go of her. He removed the steaks from the grill. "I'm merely supplementing her diet. Unless I'm mistaken, Figaro is going to have a litter of kittens in the near future." He pointed toward the lilac bush. "Right now, she's staking a claim to your take-me-back-and-keep-me present. Do you mind?"

"Hogan used to bring her gifts. Maybe she has you confused with him."

"As long as she's the only one around here that's confused about who she loves, I don't mind."

Figaro backed out from under the bushes dragging a stuffed velvet alligator by the tail. One good look at what she'd unwrapped and she arched her back; her tail bristled. The perplexed expression on her face as she bounded across the yard had Angelica and Rob holding on to each other in laughter. She climbed straight up Rob's pant leg and wedged herself between them.

"She's not sleeping with us," Angelica said as she saw green fires kindle in Rob's eyes. "She can eat my steak and steal my gifts, but I'm not sharing you with her in bed."

"Hear that, cat?"

Figaro blinked one eye at him.

"Cats can't wink!"

Angelica grinned. "Nope, but Hogan could."

"He taught her how to wink? C'mon, sweetheart, I don't believe that."

"It's true."

She detached Figaro's claws from Rob's shirt and gently dropped her to the ground. Taking him by the hand, she led him straight to the bedroom. Rob firmly closed the door behind them—as Angelica had said, this was one thing they wouldn't share with Figaro.

The telephone jangled before Angelica unfastened the top button of her dress. "I have to answer it. It could be an emergency call. I'll make it quick."

"I won't," Rob mouthed, following her to the bedside table and slowly unbuttoning her dress with his lips.

Between giggles, she said, "Franklin residence."

"Angelica Franklin?"

"Yes."

"I'm Olivia, Rob's secretary. Is he there?"

The groan she emitted wasn't a result of Rob's tongue tickling across her ribs. "It's for you."

"Me?" Rob took the receiver from her hand.

"It's your secretary."

His brow drew into a straight line. He held the phone so Angelica could hear. "Olivia?"

"I booked my cruise reservations. We both got our promotions!"

"There must be some mistake." He nuzzled Angelica's neck to reassure her that he wouldn't be going back to New York.

"No mistake. The shrink said you're undoubtedly the most creative, ingenious man she's tested. Earl's fit to be tied because he can't locate you."

"Good. Tell him I quit before he fires me. Bye, Olivia. Enjoy your cruise." He dropped the phone back in the cradle. "Now, where was I?"

"Here." Angelica pointed to her ribs, loving him to the nth degree. "Here, too."

He'd barely had a chance to unbuckle her belt when the phone rang again.

"Don't answer it," he whispered.

"Rob..." she protested.

He picked it up for her. "Rob Emery, don't you dare hang up!" Earl bellowed. "You can't resign! You've just been named vice president in charge of filmed commercials."

"I can and have, Earl. I'll call you back in a week or two. I'm busy right now."

"Dammit! We're opening offices in Orlando! You'll be working at those fancy new studios...."

Angelica snuggled against Rob as Earl promised him everything but a set of Mickey Mouse ears. Lifting her mouth to his, she whispered, "I love you. I want you to be all you can be. It's the only way you'll be happy."

"Rob! Are you there?"

"Yeah. I'm here." He peppered kisses along Angelica's neck. "Like I said, I'm very, very busy."

"Call me tomorrow?"

"Yeah, tomorrow. Bye." He hung up the phone, grinning from ear to ear. "Somebody ought to tell him that tomorrows never come. There's only the here and now."

"You're going to take his offer, aren't you?"

His hands slipped her dress off her shoulders. "Maybe. I have more important things on my mind than accepting or rejecting a job offer."

"Such as?"
"Kissing the freckle on your back . . ."

*   *   *   *   *

SILHOUETTE
Desire™

COMING NEXT MONTH

#565 TIME ENOUGH FOR LOVE—Carole Buck
Career blazers Doug and Amy Hilliard were *just too busy* . . . until they traded the big city winds for the cool country breezes and discovered the heat of their rekindled passion.

#566 BABE IN THE WOODS—Jackie Merritt
When city-woman Eden Harcourt got stranded in a mountain cabin with Devlin Stryker, she found him infuriating—infuriatingly *sexy!* This cowboy was trouble from the word go!

#567 TAKE THE RISK—Susan Meier
Traditional Caitlin Petrunak wasn't ready to take chances with a maverick like Michael Flannery. Could this handsome charmer convince Caitlin to break out of her shell and risk all for love?

#568 MIXED MESSAGES—Linda Lael Miller
Famous journalist Mark Holbrook thought love and marriage were yesterday's news. But newcomer Carly Barnett knew better—and together they made sizzling headlines of their own!

#569 WRONG ADDRESS, RIGHT PLACE—Lass Small
Linda Parsons hated lies, and Mitch Roads had told her a whopper. Could this rugged oilman argue his way out of the predicament . . . or should he let love do all the talking?

#570 KISS ME KATE—Helen Myers
May's *Man of the Month* Giles Channing thought Southern belle Kate Beaumont was just another spoiled brat. But beneath her unmanageable exterior was a loving woman waiting to be tamed.

AVAILABLE NOW:

#559 SUNSHINE
Jo Ann Algermissen

#560 GUILTY SECRETS
Laura Leone

#561 THE HIDDEN PEARL
Celeste Hamilton

#562 LADIES' MAN
Raye Morgan

#563 KING OF THE MOUNTAIN
Joyce Thies

#564 SCANDAL'S CHILD
Ann Major

SILHOUETTE DESIRE™
presents
AUNT EUGENIA'S TREASURES
by CELESTE HAMILTON

Liz, Cassandra and Maggie are the honored recipients of Aunt Eugenia's heirloom jewels...but Eugenia knows the real prizes are the young women themselves. Read about Aunt Eugenia's quest to find them everlasting love. Each book shines on its own, but together, they're priceless!

Available in December:
THE DIAMOND'S SPARKLE (SD #537)

Altruistic Liz Patterson wants nothing to do with Nathan Hollister, but as the fast-lane PR man tells Liz, love is something he's willing to take *very* slowly.

Available in February:
RUBY FIRE (SD #549)

Impulsive Cassandra Martin returns from her travels... ready to rekindle the flame with the man she never forgot, Daniel O'Grady.

Available in April:
THE HIDDEN PEARL (SD #561)

Cautious Maggie O'Grady comes out of her shell...and glows in the precious warmth of love when brazen Jonah Pendleton moves in next door.

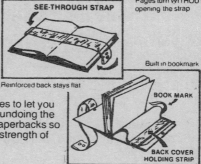

SILHOUETTE® *Desire*

MAN OF THE MONTH

SCANDAL'S CHILD
ANN MAJOR

When passion and fate intertwine...

Garret Cagan and Noelle Martin had grown up together in the mysterious bayous of Louisiana. Fate had wrenched them apart, but now Noelle had returned. Garret was determined to resist her sensual allure, but he hadn't reckoned on his desire for the beautiful scandal's child.

Don't miss SCANDAL'S CHILD by Ann Major, Book Five in the Children of Destiny Series, available now at your favorite retail outlet.